# UPROOTED
## AND
# THRIVING

one man's journey from Afghanistan
to becoming a Canadian

BARI EMAM

Tellwell Talent
www.tellwell.ca

ISBN
978-0-2288-0996-8 (Hardcover)
978-0-2288-0995-1 (Paperback)
978-0-2288-0997-5 (eBook)

# TABLE OF CONTENTS

# DEDICATION

I dedicate this book to the memory of the millions of people around the world whose lives have perished due to war, and to honour the millions of refugees and displaced people who continue to be uprooted because war is imposed upon them by those who don't value humanity. Despite the uncertain future, these souls exemplify ultimate courage and resilience by waking up everyday and trying to survive against all odds. Their spirit to move on and persevere in the face of adversity is a true example of human resilience and a lesson to us all.

# ACKNOWLEDGEMENTS

Thank you to every living being I ever met in my life. I learned something from each one of you.

I owe a great deal of appreciation to every person who believed in me and supported me in any capacity throughout my life; you gave me the strength to push beyond any obstacle and persevere in the face of adversity no matter what life threw at me. My love for you all is eternal.

I would also like to acknowledge that the land on which I now live is the traditional, unceded territory of the Kwikwetlem, Musqueam, Squamish, Sto lo, and Tsleil-Waututh First Nations.

I am indebted to the Indigenous Peoples of Canada whose territory I have inhabited since my arrival in this country in 1990. I feel that the unjust treatment of Indigenous Peoples since the formation of Canada must be talked about in explicit ways. As an immigrant from a far away land, I have benefited a great deal from all that is good about Canada. I invite everyone who calls Canada home to remember one important fact about this country's history: No matter who you are, what part of the world you come from, and how much you have contributed to improving our way of life, we all occupy a land which was taken away from the Indigenous Peoples by force. At a minimum, we have a duty to treat Canada's Indigenous Peoples with compassion, respect, and admiration for the efforts in preserving their way of life and showing resilience. I honour your way of life and stand with you in solidarity.

# INTRODUCTION

I waited thirty years to tell my story. Since my arrival
in Canada in 1990 at the age of seventeen, I knew
that the story of who I was, where I came from, and
how my family and I had gotten to Canada from
war-torn Afghanistan would be worth telling. The
uniqueness of my story is that I experienced turmoil
as a child of war and then later chose a career in
a peaceful country where war has never been a
threat, yet human struggles continued to present
themselves as part of life. I experienced that lack of
human connection is often the only thing missing
when it comes to better understanding the world we
live in. Many of the terrible things I experienced in
Afghanistan and, later, in Canada were due to a lack
of human connection. We take comfort in distances
and borders as a way of keeping ourselves safe from
the unknown, yet once we get to know others and
see them as humans first, then there will be no such
thing as the unknown. We can feel safe knowing
that those who live in all corners of the world are
not that different from us, and that most of them are
doing the best they can with what they have under

the circumstances. I just needed to be in a space and time in my life where I could tell the story.

As the years went by, I wondered: would it help both Canadians and those who eventually become Canadian if they knew each other better? Would we be better off if we heard the stories of those who have come to Canada with broken hearts and are trying to piece them together in their new homeland as they strive to be good Canadians? The more I asked myself these questions and the more time I spent living in and travelling across Canada, especially in recent years, the more convinced I became that there is a missing link and that, to help fill it, I must tell my story.

One of my biggest motivators is, at the time of writing, the current ugly, divisive global political climate, which has provoked deep racism and hatred. I started thinking that if we, as Canadians, don't come together and understand each other better, the politics of fear may take over here as well and by then, it may be too late. Once created, healing the wounds which cause division and lack of trust among people becomes very difficult, and, as we have seen in many parts of the world, this eventually tears countries apart.

I also met many immigrants in the past thirty years who, like me, worked hard to build a life for themselves in an honest way, all of whom genuinely care about their new homeland. The rhetoric of the moocher immigrant is one I have always fought against and will continue to do so. It is true that those who initially immigrate to Canada with little means can benefit from financial assistance at the expense of the Canadian taxpayers. However, just like my family, there are millions of people whose children are now a powerful contributing factor to the success of the Canadian economy and way of life. They enrich Canada and are responsible for helping many others as they become part of Canada's fabric. Their contributions are often far beyond the little funds their families initially received from the taxpayers.

Furthermore, my professional life as a police officer gave me a unique opportunity to witness a very intimate part of the lives of Canadians. After nearly two decades and investigating just about every type of crime, ranging from minor to most serious types of crimes (including over 100 murders), Canadians from all walks have shared their saddest, darkest, most shameful, and worst times with me. I have been in hospital emergency rooms to investigate shootings. I have been in the homes of families to tell them that their sons or daughters had just been murdered. I have interviewed and interrogated hundreds of people, spoken with victims of crimes and those accused of committing a crime. I interacted with Canadians of all socio-economic groups, ethnic backgrounds, cultures, religions, beliefs, genders, sexual orientations, and political views, and got to know many of them in a deep and meaningful way. I spent many years having a uniquely intimate window into the lives of Canadians. Being a person who witnessed the worse in what people are capable of in two very different countries gave me a unique dual perspective. I wanted to share the lessons I learned from seeing the world thorough my lens in an attempt to bring these lessons to life for those who have never seen or are not likely to ever experience life the way I did.

My birth country, Afghanistan, has been in the spotlight for decades, mostly due to the war and destruction that has taken place there. Before 1979, Afghanistan was known to the world as a small country with a rich history. It was a place to visit, just like many other countries whose history goes back thousands of years. The fact that such a little country even exists independently while surrounded by the former Soviet Union to the north, China to the east, Iran to the west, and Pakistan to the south is an interesting yet complicated discussion on its own. As part of the old Persian Empire, the Silk Road and being near some of the highest mountains in the world, Afghanistan's geography has fascinated many people around the world.

Unfortunately, much of the world's knowledge about Afghanistan in the past forty years has to do with wars. In 1979, the Soviet-Afghan war broke out. A decade later, Afghanistan helped break the Soviet Union's back and contributed to defeating communism; this war was fought with western money and Afghan blood. The decade of war and destruction during the Soviet occupation left Afghanistan, whose population at the time was under 30 million, with over a million killed, hundreds of thousands wounded, and about five million driven away from their homes as refugees. My family was one of those five million; we left in 1988. Communism fell apart indeed, and the world forgot about Afghanistan for about ten years before it returned to the spotlight in the September 11th attacks on the US, in 2001. Another war ensued. I was, at the time, working my first year as a police officer in Canada.

As the bombs were dropped on Afghanistan by the US Air Force and other NATO countries and leveled what was left of the country, I tried to understand. Terrorism was not born in Afghanistan, and I was not optimistic that it would die there. I worried about innocent Afghans being killed, which was hard to bear. To this day, the war on terrorism continues and the terrorist ideology has moved to other parts of the world. So why did all those people have to die?

And so, I also chose to tell this story because I did not want to accept that war, violence, and destruction are the only things that Canadians should associate with those coming from war-torn countries. I wanted Canadians to see that despite seeing horrible things and living through a war, what's in our heads and our hearts is what really matters—we are not all that different than any other Canadian. I also wanted Canadians to know that immigrants like me do become part of the fabric of our society and make our country stronger because of what we have been through. Having spent most of my life in Canada now, I know that many of those who have experienced hardships dedicate and contribute above and beyond the average citizen, because they appreciate peace and a second chance in life.

I am convinced that, by trying to understand each other—no matter where we come from—fear and negativity toward others who are not like us can become a thing of the past. I hope that by reading my story, both Canadians and those who are new to Canada appreciate the importance of connecting. I believe that the human connection is the first step towards the recognition of a universal truth about us all, no matter where we live. This universal truth is that we are not immortal, so before our time comes to check out, we need to ask ourselves: did we ever try to see others as we see ourselves, and did we make meaningful connections with others? Or did we just look at them as those who crowd our space?

I think that if we don't help ourselves find the compassion that we are all capable of, we miss an opportunity to show our human side while living. I found that, in my job as a police officer and life as a Canadian, making a genuine effort to understand others, respect them as humans, and remove the cloud of judgement is the only positive way forward. I also found that trust develops once we start looking at ourselves as complex beings who constantly need to improve. No one thing, person, country or way of life can ever claim to be perfect. Our strength is in our integration. Connect with people at a human level and you will get the best of them.

# CHAPTER 1

# My First Home

## A faint memory of peace

Children who grew up in countries such as Canada and other peaceful countries around the world have childhood memories that are often joyful and free of worry. Their stories reflect childhood as it should be. The childhood of children from war-torn countries is anything but ordinary—they are robbed of their childhood.

I was born to a loving mother who took care of four energetic children while making sure that she cooked sumptuous meals seemingly without any effort, and a firm yet gentle father whose authority I was never tempted to question, but rather accepted as the head of our family. I had a sister who was a year younger than me, a brother five years younger, and a second sister ten years younger. We played peacefully inside of our yard for hours and had a sense of togetherness and harmony despite all the little issues between siblings that are part of every family's life. However, if one of us got hurt or needed help, we all ran to their aid and this sense of being a team became a source of strength for us all as we saw much more than we expected to see and went through more than we expected to go through as children. I lived the very early part of my life in a country that once was peaceful, and I still have faint memories of Afghanistan's peaceful and joyous time-it was part of my reality until it was taken away from us by the Soviet invasion in 1979.

During warm summer nights, when the clear skies allow you to see the stars and the moon offers just enough light to set the mood for a perfect evening, we ate dinner on the large deck in front of our home, which was surrounded by the smell of roses. Dinners were even more special when family visited us in our house in Kabul. Then, my father would spray the surrounding areas of the deck and the rose bushes with cool water so that the aromas of nature would surface and add to the enjoyment of food and company. Traditional handmade Afghan carpets were laid on the ground with comfortable mattresses and pillows on their edges. This made for a cozy and comfortable seating for the young and the old, and everyone in between. Having not had dinner while sitting on the ground for almost three decades now, comfort is not the first thing that comes to mind when I think of it, but I wonder if the tradition of sitting on the ground for dinner was a way for everyone to relax and be grounded while enjoying a meal. Talking, laughing, and telling stories was part of the process when having dinner at our house with loved ones. There was a sense of unspoken gratitude for being together, in good health, and for enjoying a meal.

A typical dinner with our family would take two to three hours; no one looked at a clock nor did anyone care to know what time it was. No matter how hungry we were, we never rushed eating. Traditionally, everyone would sit on their mattresses around the rectangular carpet and one of the kids would walk around with a pot of warm water in one hand and an empty bowl in the other. These pots were normally silver-plated and decorated and almost each household had a set. The youngest kids would walk from person to person, starting with the elders, and everyone would wash their hands in preparation for dinner. Another young person would follow with a towel for drying hands. This was a common ritual across Afghanistan.

The delicious meal was prepared by my mother, grandmother, and any other female relatives who had come to visit us. Family always rolled up their sleeves to help with the cooking and serving of the food; there was no such thing as formalities. There would be a wide variety of traditional Afghani dishes such as rice, a variety of meats, vegetables, and, of course, bread. Dinner was a slow process and unfolded this way every time we had family visiting. There were no TV dinners, no sandwiches, no takeout food, and no food deliveries. I never knew about any of these things and could not imagine eating dinner any other way until we moved to Canada. For me, dinner was something that happened in the evening, when no one was in a hurry to leave and when people had let go of their tasks and chores for the day—no one ever rushed the dinner experience.

Tea, sweets, and fruits followed dinner, and this would take place in an even more relaxed way. We would sit on the carpet playing a board game and listening to the rich and informative conversations of our family members, who would be discussing topics ranging from world history to music, art, poetry, family values, and sometimes reading famous Persian poetry by Hafez Shirazi and Rumi. Many well-known Afghan artists, such as the late Ahmad Zahir, and many other wonderful and talented Afghani singers used these books, full of meaningful poetry, to sing beautiful songs which remain timeless. Much of my understanding about Afghani music and the meaning of the poems sang by Afghani and Iranian artists came from listening to my parents and grandparents discussing them. The beautiful and rich stories, combined with skilful composition, always captured my attention and no matter what I was going through in life, the music of my heritage remained with me. I used this gift to draw upon as a source of enjoyment and took comfort in listening to Afghani songs while reflecting about many aspects of my life. For this I owe a great deal of gratitude to the poets, artists, and everyone who was behind producing such wonderful music. I found that few things in life moved me as much as the heartfelt music of my birthplace.

By this time, everyone was either lying on their mattresses or leaning on a pillow. The wonderful thing about this was that we knew our evening would continue until we were ready for bed and when bedtime came, our mattresses and pillows were right there. Falling asleep under the stars was not something I had to wait for a vacation to experience; as I got tired, the evening was starting to cool down to the perfect temperature, when the fresh air was all that was left to breathe and the peace and quiet fell upon the city, allowing us to sleep peacefully with the moon as our night light. I don't remember taking a vacation as a child. Why would we need a vacation if the norm was to enjoy life and not wait to connect with nature? The notion of having to get away from the everyday hustle and bustle of life and go on a vacation was something new to me as we entered our life in Canada.

The long and enjoyable meal would not be complete without the oldest person—sitting at the head of the carpet—saying a long and heartfelt prayer. Since we were all sitting on the ground, there was no head seat at the table, so anywhere the most senior person in the family sat ended up being the head of the carpet. Our great-grandmother, who could not read or write, was the eldest, and, with four generations sitting on the ground with her, she knew that when it was prayer time, we all looked to her for wisdom. She would use simple words and say the prayer in a calm voice and beautiful tone while we sat in such complete silence that we could hear even a single bird flying over us. The silence was a sign of respect for our great-grandmother and for the prayer itself. She would normally thank our Creator for all that we had and everyone whom we had in our family and, most importantly, reminded us to take this moment presented to us as a gift. She would also always say a prayer to our late ancestors and, lastly, wish peace and prosperity for all. My great-grandmother taught me at a very early age to be grateful for every moment—after all, the only certainty was the moment we had, for what might come and what might be is not in our hands. This life lesson was further cemented during my life. Staying true to this simple teaching makes of a person a solid rock. So, no matter what life has brought, these simple values have been a solid rock for me to lean on and anchor myself against.

My great-grandmother and grandparents would often share stories about our ancestors and places across Afghanistan. My father, who had spent some twenty years of his youth studying then working in New York, would turn the radio to *The Voice of America* or the BBC. America and England seemed like such far away countries, and hearing the Americans or the British on the radio was as close as I thought I would ever get to such places. Most of my knowledge about America came from my father, who told me about the sounds and sights of Broadway, Hollywood movies, and the music of that era, which to this day has a large audience. Our home in Kabul in the 1970s sounded no different than a home in Canada or the US—the voices of Frank Sinatra, Dean Martin, Nat King Cole, Bob Hope, and many other American entertainers from my Dad's record collection flowing through the house like a refreshing breeze on a warm day. This way, my father brought the west, especially America, into our home. He also created a library in our home, which included encyclopaedias and novels. As a child in Kabul, I read Ernest Hemingway's *The Old Man and the Sea*. Dad cherished his memories of New York City and wanted us to be part of it by bringing part of American culture into our home. This was my father's way and I adopted it. As I met people from all corners of the world, I looked for the good and tried to understand, respect, and enjoy what their cultures have to offer.

Our opinion of America, and especially of New York City, was very high when I was a child. I never knew where life might take us, but I always wished that one day, I could go to New York City with my father, so that he could show me the city where he spent his best and most youthful years. This was a dream until 1994, when I found myself in New York City with my father. Dad showed me his high school, the places he worked, the historic landmarks where he spent many days and Central Park where he had eaten hundreds of meals, all by himself on one of the benches. My father was the first Afghan person to obtain an immigrant visa to the US. Others had travelled there as visitors, students, and for business, but he was the first Afghani who immigrated to the US in 1951. As I learned about the US and their history of race relations, I can only imagine some of the things my father faced as an Afghani in New York City in the 1950s, but somehow his positive outlook on life and seeing the good in all people made it a pleasant experience, and he stayed for twenty years. As we walked by Times Square, he noted the progress, the high rises, the wealth of many of the people in New York. He then emphasized that the connections we make with human beings—not material wealth—will go with us when we leave this life. He was gently teaching me to not get caught up in the material world and to not forget who I was. This lesson carried me during challenging times in life. I also learned that, despite reflecting on all the good times he had in New York, Dad loved his country of origin and this is why he returned to Afghanistan after living there for twenty years.

Now, even though I do not remember much about peaceful Afghanistan, I remember enough to be able to relate to those who have emigrated.

## One night of heavy planes in the skies

On a cold Kabul night, when the snow blanketed the city just enough to brighten the sky, the Soviet government gave the Afghan people a Christmas present. For an entire night, I heard heavy cargo planes flying over the skies of Kabul, something that I had never heard before in my life. While Afghanistan was sleeping, the Soviet Union flew in several hundreds of thousands of troops, which, in a matter of hours, overturned the government. By daybreak on Christmas Day in 1979, Afghanistan was occupied. After leaving for work the next morning just like any other day, my father came back home much earlier than usual. Dad's facial expression reflected a look as if he had seen a ghost. And he had, the ghost being Soviet soldiers and their tanks, who had taken over the streets of Kabul. Dad described them as young and scared-looking soldiers who seemed lost. This was the beginning of a ten-year occupation, which sent Afghanistan into a state of turmoil for decades to come.

I was about six years old at the time of the Soviet invasion and all I remember was that my parents talked about it a lot. Their voices and faces spoke louder than their words; they seemed sad, disillusioned, and worried. I, on the other hand, was excited to see tanks on the streets because I had never seen them before and was curious about what a Soviet soldier looked like. So, starting the next day, every time I heard a loud noise, thinking that it may be a tank, I ran out to the edge of our yard to catch a glimpse. I saw the tanks and heard the loud noise they made, saw how fast they went, the cloud of dust left behind. I hoped that one day I could talk to the Soviet soldiers.

Those tanks and the faces of Soviet soldiers later became one of the ugliest sights to me; to this day, the look and sound of a tank and those of an attack-style Apache helicopter make me shiver. As for the Soviet soldiers, I have learned to think of them as scared young boys who were duped and pushed into a war they did not want to be in. They committed atrocities in Afghanistan that are hard to forgive, but they were used as tools to advance an agenda well beyond their knowledge and power.

The natural reaction of the Afghan people, to rebel against the occupation, led to ten years of death and destruction during which I learned a lot about humanity and the value of human life. As I was getting older, my parents and the news from the same radio channels my father listened to portrayed the reality of what was unfolding. The puppet pro-Soviet government in Kabul was propagating the story of the new and "democratic" government being all about making life better for Afghans. At the same time, the rebels had risen against the Soviets in villages and countryside all over Afghanistan. They were called "freedom fighters" by the western world and their images were being broadcast on televisions, printed in magazines and newspapers all over the western world as brave warriors who were not afraid to fight a superpower. The evils of war also slowly started to creep into our daily lives in Kabul.

## A child's scary walk to school

The narrow and unpaved streets of Kabul in the 1980s were neither ready nor designed for the Soviet tanks that tore them to shreds as their steel belts ripped through the streets in a violently loud roar, shaking the walls of homes they passed. This was a daily thing. I was not so worried about the shaking of the walls and the torn-apart roads—it was facing the tanks on foot that concerned me.

My younger sister and I would finish our breakfast, pack our books and folding chairs—our school was too poor to provide furniture for every child. My father had tried to find the lightest and smallest possible chairs for us to carry back and forth between home and school. Our walk to school took about twenty minutes. Each morning, we would carefully walk together while holding hands and hugging the walls, looking and listening for tanks. I was eight years old then, and a tank was as big as a house to me. It made a terrifying noise as it went by, created dust that we would breathe in, and armed Soviet soldiers sat on top of them holding machine guns.

My sister, who was a year younger than me, only looked at me as a tank was about to go by us. No words would be spoken but her little hand would squeeze my hand—as if her eight-year-old big brother would somehow protect her from a fifty-tonne tank. I often thought about a tank hitting us; there would be nothing left of us, and I wondered: How would our parents know what happened to us? Who would tell them? Would we even be recognizable?

As we finally made it to school—which focused on pro-Soviet material—we would feel a bit safer than we did on the walk to school. But as the years went by, this safety was also taken away.

Aside from the deplorable physical condition of the schools, the war-torn state of the country in the 1980s afforded a teacher in Kabul the right to physically assault a student who did not provide the correct answer, had not done homework, or showed any disrespect toward the teacher. My sister and I did our best to not put ourselves in a position in which we would be hit, but we got hit anyway. If a teacher was absent for a day, or part of a day, there was no contingency plan in place, so a classroom full of children would be left to manage themselves. A principal or someone from the school would walk in just to say that the students should stay quiet, read, or occupy themselves somehow, and then simply leave. We were small children, and eventually we would be making so much ruckus that someone from the school would come in holding a tree branch, ready to punish all the students in the classroom. We would all have to stand up, hold the palms of our hands up and the principal or the teacher who was sent to control the classroom would start to hit each child in the palm of both hands. The number of strikes and how hard they hit us depended on how angry this person was that day. Not everyday was this bad and not every teacher carried themselves in such disgraceful way, however, just having a few of such days was enough to leave children with bad memories about school. I always thought that children deserved much better despite the ongoing struggles in the country.

It was not until I started school in Canada as a Grade 10 student that I experienced a different educational standard and realized even more how cruel the practice of punishing children was. As a high school student, the most I ever saw a teacher do was to send a student to the principal's office, typically for good reason. I had immense respect for my teachers in Canada and still have for all those who make learning for children a fun and rewarding experience.

## Getting groceries while dodging bullets

By the age of nine, I was helping my father with the morning grocery run before I went to school every day. My father's emphasis on giving his family and children the best he could included taking me with him to the row of grocery stores near the main road close to our home. Dad would purchase the freshest groceries for the day, and it was my job to walk back home with them as he went off to work.

On a beautiful spring morning, the sky bright, the sun not fully out from behind the mountains just behind our home, I was holding grocery bags when I heard gunshots. My heart clenched, and my palms started sweating; one would think I would be used to the sound by now, but that wasn't the case. Machine guns were being fired in the mountain; their sound was quite rapidly moving down towards the main road. Terrified, people were scattering everywhere, taking cover as best they could. I knew I had to do the same; I ran to the closest wall and dove behind it as the gunfire became even more intense. Bullets struck the unpaved road behind me, making their presence known with a cloud of dust. The sudden disorganised and panicked movement of thick crowd of people made some of them freeze.

This was the first time I came so close to being hit by a bullet. The fear and panic fed on themselves, bringing about more fear and panic. No one knew where to hide or what to do; one man, hit in the leg, was limping towards a tree in a desperate bid for cover. Despite the war, I had, until then, never seen a crowd faced with gunfire nor a person being hit by a bullet. I still don't know what happened that day, who was shooting at whom and why. Unfortunately, incidents like this became a way of life in Kabul and I developed an ear for recognizing how close or far the gunfire was.

The divisive politics and the destruction sent Afghanistan back a few decades. My father had left New York City in the hope of raising a family in his homeland and he had brought so many good things from America and the Western world—the disappointment of arrival of the dark ages was evident in his face, words, and actions. Despite this, he remained hopeful for almost a decade. Leaving our roots, which had grown strong in Afghanistan for many generations, was not something he wanted to think about. This changed when the violence came close to us and affected our daily lives.

## A day at school where rockets fell

By the mid 1980's, my sister and I were attending the same school and had become good at avoiding tanks. If caught in a crossfire, we would seek cover as best as we could and leave the rest up to faith. We were not prepared for the next level of violence—rocket attacks as the rebels closed in on Kabul. The weapons the rebels received from the US and other western countries enabled them to fire off these rockets from areas just outside of Kabul. The rebels did not target a specific army or government facilities—they struck anything and killed anyone, creating a sense of terror in Kabul. Residents fled the city, making the puppet Kabul government weak and ineffective. Eventually, this worked in favor of the rebels.

One summer afternoon, with the warm Kabul sun shining, the blasts of rockets interrupted the relative peace. By this time, most children in Kabul knew which sounds belonged to which weapons and how close they were. My classmates and the teacher were in a state of terror; the destruction of our school and likelihood of serious injury or death were the only things to think about. The sound of rockets came closer and closer. Some children were praying, and so was I. Then, a deafening explosion as the rocket landed just outside our school, shaking us like stones in a pothole. We screamed as another rocket hit. Our teacher looked at all the innocent and frightened faces of her students and said: "Run home. May God keep you all."

The next day, we went back to school. The rockets had landed just outside the school walls. The hole in the ground was as big as a car. School became a place of fear and anxiety, but we continued to go, and chased after each other in the school yard, playing and laughing while under constant threat of dying. What choice did we have?

After these early experiences in life, I became unafraid of anyone or anything. My belief in a higher power and predetermined events in life also grew stronger after these experiences. War or no war, I was not afraid. I realized that worrying about being killed every day would mean living my life in fear and I simply decided that I would not be fearful of anything anymore.

## Why is our house getting hit by bullets?

It was a cold fall night in Kabul where the darkness came upon the city quicker and everyone warmed up their homes a little earlier as the days shortened. The sun would sit on the mountains of Paghman, one of Afghanistan's most beautiful places to visit. Our home had a perfect view of the Paghman Mountains. Fall in Kabul is beautiful and crisp, the sky always blue, some clouds rolling in from time to time and the sun slowly disappearing from the city behind the mountains of Paghman. The quiet in the city was disturbed occasionally by gunshots or flares, which were fired by police or the military to let each other know where they were or create light in the darkness of alleys and streets of Kabul during their patrols. We grew accustomed to such sounds.

Up to this point, our home had been safe from both the rebels or the Soviets because the majority of fighting was taking place in the outskirts of Kabul and the rebels had not yet gotten close to the city center. Our home was heated by a woodburning stove and we all used the largest room in the house as our bedroom. As we went to bed, the stove would give off just enough light to act as our bedtime light. Our home was custom built from concrete by a friend of my father upon his return from the US in the early 70s and we felt safe in it. The front of our house faced the Paghman mountains. In the summer, I would go up on the roof of the house just to take in the view and could see the valley just below the mountains, including the beautiful fields of corn. In Kabul and many other parts of Afghanistan, having fruit trees in yards is very common. We had a mini orchard with grape, peach, apple, and even walnut trees. Tall trees surrounded the sides of our home. We had many rooms facing the front of the house with many windows overlooking a large deck at the front of the house and plenty of yard space. During the day, we used all parts of the house. Us kids were running in and out of the house all day but mostly playing outside until it was dinnertime. It was not until the war began that we started to stay together in one room at night for dinner and sleep. We did this for two reasons; firstly, there were regular blackouts in Kabul during which we would not have power for many days, making it difficult for a family to keep an entire house warm and lit during the night. Secondly, the room at the very back of the house seemed the safest, as it was blocked by our living room walls. Normally, gunfire erupted much more during the night than it did at daytime, so we felt a little safer from bullets there.

One evening of September 1985, a sudden burst of energy filled my little brother just as bedtime was approaching. The little energy-laden child started running around, grinning, happy, being a silly, adorable fool like so many others of his age. The bed became the recipient of his energetic joy; my little brother launched himself on it and started gleefully jumping up and down on his mattress. And, as had happened since the dawn of time—or at least, since the dawn of mattresses—our mother's stern rebuke made him lie down in his bed only seconds before we were startled by sound of gunfire, seemingly from right outside our house. Bullets were hitting our home and I heard concrete falling and glass breaking. I had heard stories of people being killed in their homes by the rebels or the Soviets, that sometimes-Soviet soldiers would get drunk and open fire at random homes and even break doors down to take what they wanted. All these thoughts rushed through my head as bullets continued to strike our home.

My mother's actions that night saved my little brother's life. Many bullets struck the house that night. It stopped eventually, but we stayed on the ground, the room so quiet that we could her each other breathing. I was sweating from fear and could not stop thinking about people with guns coming into our home. My earlier promise to myself that I would no longer be afraid of anything did not work too well. That night somehow went by and slowly dawn arrived. It was not fully light yet, but my mom found a bullet hole on our inside wall. The bullet hole was where my little brother's head had been when he was jumping up and down on his bed earlier in the night.

As darkness faded, we saw many other bullet holes, shattered windows, and other damage. We counted ourselves lucky that day and continued on with daily life. To this day we talk about that night and how my brother—a little boy then and a father of two at the time of writing—was so lucky to have lived that night.

I am full of emotions as I wrote the paragraphs above while sitting at my dining-room table. At this very moment, I hear fireworks. It is Halloween night and I am in Canada. I am having a drink as I type away; the sound of fireworks to me is the sound of joy and celebration, my children are in bed and I have no concerns. What a difference a piece of land makes, the only difference I see between my children and those who live in war-torn countries. My lucky children just happen to be far enough from war. In times like these, my sense of gratitude is magnified. We are here, enjoying peace and prosperity, while some children who are stuck in a war zone are shaking with fear every time, they hear an explosion or gunfire. Are we any better than them? Are we more human than they are?

## Why is life not valued in a war-torn country?

Becoming a police officer and investigating homicides was not the career I had in mind at the age of thirteen while living in Kabul. But maybe there was a foreshadowing when I found myself so close to one of the greatest tragedies that takes place among humans in all corners of the world. I never understood or accepted the murder of a human being at the hands of another, no matter what the reasons were. I looked at it this way: the most intelligent species on earth should have enough good sense and the emotional intelligence to stop themselves or anyone else from ever killing a human. It took me about a decade while I was in my thirties investigating over one hundred homicides in Canada to understand the complexities that result in this type of a tragedy and all the lives it affects.

My views on humans, their abilities to commit horrific acts, the trail of destruction left behind because of such acts, and their lack of humanity shaped most of my belief system from a younger age. I would compare killers to animals and say things like, even in the animal kingdom, the killing of another is usually the means to the end of survival by consuming the dead animal as food, so why do humans kill? What's there to be gained? And how can people not have the ability to find another way and resort to murder? As my life unfolded in a way more unique than I ever thought it would, many of these questions were answered as I became a homicide investigator many years later.

It was in 1986 and I had just turned thirteen. While playing in our yard on a frosty winter day, when the snow fully covered the mountain tops surrounding Kabul and the sun was reflecting against the icy mountains, making it difficult to stare at them, my brother and I would play all day in our front yard. The crisp air was refreshing and, even though it was cold, we played outside most of the day. As the war continued in Afghanistan, playing outside of our yard was unsafe, but we felt safe playing in the yard. Winters in Kabul were especially fun because schools were closed. Winter in Kabul was like the summer holidays for kids in North America. My brother and I would spend so much time outside that we would have to get too cold or too hungry to notice that we had spend several hours playing out in the wintry weather.

Homes in Kabul were almost exclusively surrounded by walls, which were about five to six feet tall; this is how properties were normally divided from each other and fenced off from the street. Our home was on a slope, so looking over the walls of our yard gave us an unobstructed view of the street. One winter day, something happened, and this incident became one of my main motivators in life to seek justice for those who cannot defend themselves. I used this passion to strengthen my abilities as a police officer in Canada, where I investigated crimes against persons including homicides for many years.

On that chilly day, my little brother and I were outside, as we often were, playing and watching the colourful kites against the blue sky as they were often flown by young and old from various locations. These were the usual innocent and fun activities of children our age. We were interrupted by the sounds of a loud argument that seemed to be happening right in front of our house. Curious, my little brother ran to me. He was too small to see over the yard wall and called me over to see what the commotion was all about. He initially wanted me to give him a boost to see first-hand what was happening, but from the yelling and the tone of the voices, I knew that these were angry men. Luckily, I denied my brother's request to let him have the first look. As I peered over our wall to see what was happening, I saw that the two angry men were a policeman and a soldier.

I told my brother that this was not a big deal, as both men are in police and military uniforms and are likely going to sort this out. Both men were very young; the solider was about eighteen or nineteen years old and the policeman seemed a few years older. The Soviet-made Kalashnikov rifle, also known as the AK47, was the weapon of choice for the military personnel who were part of the puppet Soviet regime in Kabul. I had never seen anyone fire this gun before but seeing it on the shoulders of Afghan and Soviet soldiers made it look intimidating and I knew that the only purpose of a gun like this was to kill people. As the argument became increasingly heated, my heart started racing, until it stopped at the sight of the soldier turning his rifle toward the policeman. Surely this was just a joke, or, at most, an idle threat. Waving the rifle around threateningly, the soldier warned him that if the policeman spoke another word, he would soon be full of holes. I couldn't help but wonder if the bullets would go through the wall and hit my brother; but no, right? The walls were thick enough – right? And surely the policeman would de-escalade the fight. But, to my shock and horror, he instead said: "Go ahead." This couldn't be happening. The policeman was looking into the soldier's eyes as he raised his rifle and fired one shot, just a single one, straight into the chest of the policeman. The sound of my pounding heart filled my ears as I watched him fall to the ground.

I heard the thud of the bullet hitting the policeman in the chest. Up to this point, I had never seen a person being killed. I saw that the bullet went right through his body as he dropped on his stomach. The blood stain on the back of his shirt left just enough of a mark to show where the bullet had exited his body. The look on the soldier's face was one of shock, as if he could not believe he had just killed a man. He shouldered his rifle and ran. I only followed his movements for a short while before focusing on the policeman whose blood was now starting to fill a hole in the unpaved and snowy gravel road. The colour of his blood against the white snow grew larger as he laid motionless. His eyes remained partially open and I saw him taking his last breath. After that, I no longer saw his body move and I knew that he was gone.

I froze. I told my brother to go inside the house and stood there for a bit. I did not know what to do. As the man's lifeless body laid there, a truck drove by. The driver of the truck had to have seen the man's body, and I expected that he would stop and check on the man. To my disbelief, the driver of the truck slowed down, looked at the body then drove around him. My belief about how little a human life means in war-torn regions of the world solidified that day.

Scared about getting in trouble with my father for being so nosy and for somehow being questioned by the police, I ran inside the house and was planning on not saying anything. But the minute my father looked at my face, he knew that something was wrong. He asked: "What happened?" I walked over to him and sat beside him, then told him quietly: "I think someone was killed just outside of the front door of our home." I did not want my brother or my younger siblings to hear this; I did not want them to have yet another scary story to haunt them. Dad quietly spoke to my mother and they both hugged me. A few minutes went by and the police knocked on our door. Dad spoke with them first; they wanted to know if anyone in our house had seen or heard anything. Dad told them that he heard a single gunshot and looked at his watch and provided them with the time, he said it was exactly three o'clock in the afternoon. He then told them that I had been looking over the wall to see what was happening outside of our front door and witnessed the murder.

One of the policemen said to my Dad: "The kid will have to come with us." As I saw Dad standing there in his winter coat, casual kakis and slippers, I asked myself, What can Dad say to these guys who are at our door with guns and authority? Knowing what I had just seen, I was terrified at the thought of going anywhere with these guys. How could I trust anyone? Who cares if they say they are the police, what would they ask me? What if they don't believe me? Or worse yet, what if they force me to make up things that aren't true? My father, who never resembled a tough guy, had a very assertive side to him. Dad told the policeman: "I told you what you need to know, and my son is not coming with you guys." Dad told me to stay inside the house and walked outside with the policeman. As I watched from over the wall, my Dad's arms were flying around more and more, and he was clearly arguing with these policemen about why I had nothing more to offer them. Watching the back and forth between my unarmed father and the policemen made me nervous and I started to shake. I knew they had the power and the guns to do what they wanted to and no one would hold them accountable if they did something wrong. But despite their persistence, Dad stood his ground and did not give in. He finally convinced the policemen that I would give them a witness statement but in the presence of my father and would not go anywhere with the police except to sit inside their jeep with my Dad sitting beside me just outside of our house. As the years went by and I learned more about governments, the police and corruption in war-torn regions of the world, I understood why a parent had to be so protective of their child and not trust officials.

I remember asking the policeman about the killer and if they would kill the guy if they found him. My Dad stopped me. My knowledge as a thirteen-year-old about the complexities of a murder investigation and how the justice systems around the world dealt with such a crime was nonexistent. I thought that the only punishment for those who killed someone had to be their execution, in order to make things equal. This varied significantly from my views later in life about the barbaric nature of capital punishment and any other acts of violence against those accused of crimes.

With this experience, I thought that being a policeman must be a terrible job. Who would want to spend their life dealing with such tragic events? Seeing dead bodies, trying to figure out what happened to them—and even when they did, what good would come of it? The lives were lost, and nothing would change that. They must be crazy. At the time, I never imagined that some twenty years later and in a corner of the world far away from Kabul, where there was no war and no reason for anyone to carry a gun or kill each other, I would be the policeman knocking on people's doors while investigating homicides.

## Was I going to be another statistic?

Despite all that happened in Kabul, I knew that my parents were trying their best to stay positive about the future of the country. Yet this positivity was now turning into a fantasy. By the mid-1980s, many of our beloved young relatives were escaping the country as they were about to enter manhood, at which age they would be drafted into the Soviet-backed military. The option of escaping was the best, the Soviets were hated by most Afghans and very few Afghans wanted their children to fight and die for their cause. Because of this, young Afghan men escaped the country by the hundreds of thousands to avoid being forced to join the Afghan military. Amongst those who were able to flee were some of my cousins and second cousins, most of whom eventually immigrated to the United States or Europe. Decades later, I was reunited with some of them in the US as I travelled south of the border from Canada. Those who were unable to escape were drafted into the Afghan army. For the most part, they all felt trapped in a military that fought other Afghans and that helped the Soviets brutalize the Afghan people further.

As I neared the age of fourteen, in 1987, the basic and very bizarre method of checking my age started to creep into my life. By this time, I was in high school, which was about an hour away from our home, so I would have to walk and take a bus to get to school every day. Somewhere along my route to school, I would run into the military recruiting or military police personnel. They were among some of the most uneducated of Afghans and would harass young men constantly by asking them for identification everywhere they went. The reason for this was to identify young men who had reached the age of sixteen, who would then be drafted into the military.

A typical stop was always marked by the unexpected stop of the bus. The first ones who would be in a state of panic were the young men who were in their mid to late teens. They would change from just being a passenger on the bus to frantically looking around to see if it was the military recruiters again. Some of us would try to conceal ourselves behind the elderly and the women on the bus to see if the recruiters could just take a look at the bus through the outside windows and just let the bus go by, thinking that the stop was not worth their time. However, this didn't always work. The bus drivers were annoyed with these stops as were all the passengers, they always looked at us with sadness and concern knowing that the youth of Kabul were being targeted only to be dragged into a war they wanted nothing to do with. Just like anything else in life, the stops by the military recruiters were different each time, depending on the attitudes of the people. Some were trying to be considerate while doing their unpleasant job, but others were loud and obnoxious, showing little respect to those on board the bus and pushing their way through the crowded bus. Most people could not stand them and as they boarded the bus, I would hear comments from the passengers about how they wished these guys would just go away. People who were on their way to work and school would be annoyed about being late, and the elderly who were standing because they could not find a seat would complain of being unnecessarily detained. Almost every time a teenager would fall victim to these stops and be escorted off the bus, those who were allowed to go would all stare as the young men were taken away and then there was a certain sadness and calm inside the bus. The elderly would say prayers, and oftentimes they were the only ones who would say something like: "May god rescue us from this misery one day."

Some kids would disappear for a few days after being picked up by these characters on the streets and would come back home with a shaved head and wearing a military uniform. For their families, this was generally a surprise and most of them had no choice but to accept this as a way of life. Many of these young men would then be sent to fight against the rebel forces all over Afghanistan. Hundreds of thousands of these young Afghan men returned home in a casket. This is just one example from one country; unfortunately, almost every war-torn country experiences such injustices to this day and most people in peaceful countries are unaware that these child soldiers are one of the biggest casualties of wars around the world.

Sometimes, checking your identification was not enough for these military recruiting characters. They would question the validity of the identification because they knew that no one was willing to join the military and most young men would go to whatever extent they had to avoid being drafted into the military. If they did not believe the validity of your identification, they would ask you to roll up your pant legs to see if you were old enough to grow hair on your legs. I would think to myself, how stupid and embarrassing is this? How could we be subject to this? And lastly, would they really take me to a military base because of the hair on my legs?

The normal conversations of asking how the day went at school and what the kids learned was not the first thing my parents asked me once I returned home from school every day. The first thing they wanted to know was if my trips to and from school was interrupted by the road checks. As they asked me these questions day after day, I realized that being away from me and not knowing if I had been picked up to join the army was hard on my parents. I tried my best to relay the stories about the road checks to my parents in such a way that it would not cause them to worry too much. However, there was not much I could do to soft sell such a thing. I knew that mom and dad did not want to think about the prospect of me showing up at home one day with a shaved head and wearing a military uniform. They told me that they wanted a better life for me. But I knew that the truth was not the pursuit of a better life, but the prospects of seeing their son lying in a casket one day. This worry had become common for millions of Afghan mothers and fathers. From then on, my parents were on a mission to get me out of Afghanistan.

As the number of young men from our family who had been forced to serve in the army because they could not leave Kabul started to slowly increase, so did my parent's anxiety. One of my cousins who was forced to serve in the Afghan army was the first casualty. He was killed at a young age, his son only a few days old at the time of his death. I remember going to my aunt's house the day they returned his body to his family home. I did not know what to expect before going in but that changed quickly. As my parents and I stepped closer to the house, I could hear the loud cries of everyone inside and the whole neighbourhood knew that tragedy had struck this family. I couldn't believe what I was seeing and hearing. The sorrow in the voices of my cousins and aunt and all the family members who were there to support them was surreal. I was in shock. This is the first time I realized what every Afghan family must go through each time a young man lost his life to the senseless war imposed on the Afghan people by the Soviets. Seeing my handsome cousin's face in a casket in the middle of their living room after I had seen him well and alive only weeks earlier was a reality check for me that this war was not ending anytime soon. The sobbing by my aunt and cousins who had lost the one person they held so dearly was hardly bearable. His death left the emptiness in all our hearts which could never be filled. Unfortunately, this became a common occurrence for many Afghan families as the war went on for many years.

Our normal weekly or bi-weekly visits to my grandparents house also started to become tainted. My oldest uncle who was forced to join the Afghan army was posted just outside of Kabul to the southern border near Pakistan. He would visit my grandparents whenever he could but never once spoke about what his life was like outside of Kabul and in the army. His ability to keep the bad stories of war away from everyone was incredible to the point that he was trying to hide being shot in the leg and hip from everyone by making up a story about how he had slightly hurt himself. However, it was his concerned mother, my grandmother, who had seen his wounds as he was changing his bandages one day. I only became aware of this as my grandmother was quietly telling my mother, who was the oldest sister in the family, that her brother had been shot. Grandma and mom wiped away their tears as they discussed how my uncle did not want to tell anyone about this because he did not want to worry the family, especially the children.

Grandma, her voice shaking, also told my mother that she did not want to live to see the day when something was to happen to one of her sons. After their discussion, both grandma and mom put their brave faces on and joined the family, yet again pretending that all was well, but I knew that their worries were just getting worse. In this moment, I further learned about the love of Afghan mothers for their sons who had become sacrificial lambs for an unjust war imposed upon them. Years later, as I watched the news about American soldiers going to Iraq, I often thought about their mothers. I felt that they must have suffered in the same way as the women of Afghanistan did by watching their sons and daughters take part in an unpopular war. Stories like the above served as an added pressure for my parents to continue and find ways for me to avoid being forced in the military. And when I was about fourteen years old, my parents decided that they would not just sit there and hope for the best.

## Leaving my family behind

At the age of fourteen, my parents told me that the only way for me to be safe and get away from falling victim to partaking in the war was to leave Afghanistan. My heart started pounding; I felt dizzy, and had to take a slow, deep breath to calm myself down. My parents were, after all, only doing what they always did, what all parents did: trying their best to give the best life to their child. They probably were even more aware than I was of the dangers that awaited me, I was only a teenager. Fleeing the country all by myself was a scary prospect. But we also all knew what could potentially wait for me if I didn't: conscription, war, and either a terrible injury or death.

I couldn't help but feel angry; I was only fourteen. This was not an age for me to be thinking about how to survive. I should be thinking about school, football, girls—not death! But I couldn't let my anger take over, and especially, couldn't let my anger out on my poor parents, who were probably just as angry as I was. Or maybe even more. Dad had arranged with a relative to take me out of the country with the help of a smuggler and I would eventually end up in Pakistan with the hopes of immigrating to the United Stated. I had no idea how any of this would be possible. How I would survive? Who would I live with? How will I take care of myself? But I knew that I had to leave.

I remember that the look in my mother's eyes and my aunt who lived with us at the time was always one of sadness in the weeks leading up to my departure. Both would tear up every time they looked at me. I guess I never knew the impact this separation would have on them; they were mostly worried about how I would survive. The actual struggle of being away from home never really sunk in with me because I was so young, but many years later, I realized that my mom and aunt were heartbroken because they were about to suffer a loss and a possible separation from me for a long time... maybe forever.

Saying goodbye to my parents and siblings was the saddest part of all this. I had never been away from home since birth, unlike life in Canada, where

I have often seen the goodbyes between families who become emotional and tear up when their children move away for a while to attend school, travel, or work away from home. They all seem so ordinary to me, because there is a sense of joy attached to these types of goodbyes. Parents see their children grow and move on to experience life on their own for the first time, so they can prosper. But for me, leaving my entire family in a war zone and not knowing if I would ever see them again was an entirely different experience. This feeling of uncertainty was the biggest challenge for me. Would I ever see them again? Or would I have to figure out the rest of my life, as of the age of fourteen, without the loving guidance of my father or the tender support of my mother? I couldn't fathom it.

As I prepared to leave on a spring day, when the snow was almost all gone from our yard, I thought of this spring season as the worst one in my life. Normally, spring was a joyful season during which I would be helping my father with some gardening and digging us out of the Kabul winter. Preparing for the spring was a momentous time of the year for people in countries such as Afghanistan and Iran, as we welcomed the new year and celebrated the rebirth and rejuvenation of nature. But for me, none of this mattered this year.

In the early morning where I left home, I could hardly look into the innocent eyes of my younger siblings. They had a look of confusion in their faces and did not know why I was leaving, nor what all the tears were about. At the age of fourteen, I could not make sense of the situation, less so, I guess, could my thirteen, nine, and four year-old siblings. On the drive away from my home, I tried my hardest not to cry and kept wiping away tears as we got further and further out of the Kabul city limits. I just wanted to go back home so badly, I wished something happened that day to stop us from proceeding. We arrived in a village just outside of Kabul where we were going to wait for our guide/smuggler to take us out of the country. For the first time in my life, I met some Afghans who were not from Kabul; they did not look or talk like the people of Kabul. Not long after we arrived at this house just outside of Kabul, I started to hear the discussions; the men were talking about the fighting between the rebels and the Soviets, the condition of the areas we were expected to travel through and the risks of being either bombed by Soviet planes or shot at by the rebel forces. As these discussions took place, I realized how much worse life was for the Afghan people outside of Kabul.

Having no control or say about this journey, I continued for the next two days to think about all the possible scenarios. As the human mind tends to do, especially for a fourteen-year-old who is trying to escape a war-torn country, I began to think of all the worst-case scenarios. What if we were caught by the Soviets, who had destroyed much of Afghanistan and brutalized Afghans in villages such as the ones we were about to travel through? The Soviet-backed government was based in Kabul, which is where my family and I lived all of our lives. What if rebel fighters thought of me as being part of the communist regime? This would normally enrage them and result in taking men prisoners and could result in torture or death if they were suspected of being part of the Kabul government. All these thoughts played in my head and added to my worries to a point where I nearly broke down. Then I switched to wishful thinking, the biggest wish being that hopefully something prevents me from leaving Kabul and I would get back home to my family. I thought that no matter what happened to us, I wanted us to all be together.

The intense fighting just outside of Kabul was so bad that smugglers were advising that we go back home. I felt that the gods of wishful thinking were listening to me on that day. Suddenly the pain I was about to endure by leaving everyone who meant everything to me was about to come to an end. On our way back home, I was happy and at peace with the fact that even though I was going back towards all the dangers of living in Kabul, at least I would be with my loved ones. Entering the front door of our home and seeing the looks in my parents and siblings faces was one of relief and happiness. I knew that even though my parents wanted me to go away to save my life, they knew that sending me away alone was a mistake. We never spoke much about this after I returned home that day, but as the years went by, my parents would mention this experience from time to time and say how grateful they were that I had returned. They acknowledged that going through everything in life as a family was much easier than having one of us missing.

# CHAPTER 2

# Leaving Home

## Rockets exploding closer than before

In 1988, the year before the Soviet troops left Afghanistan, the city of Kabul became the target of heavy rocket attacks. The rebel forces started to close in on the city and were gaining ground. The fall of Kabul was imminent. The new wave of violence came in the form of rockets hitting homes in our neighbourhood. Aside from the lingering worry of me being forced to join the military, our entire family was now in harm's way. We knew that all it took was a rocket landing on our home. My parents decided to leave Kabul.

The next phase was our tearful goodbyes. Anytime a family wanted to leave Kabul, they left secretively because the pro-Soviet government was paranoid about those against them. So, the potential harm or unnecessary imprisonment of those whom they thought were supportive of the rebels or the western world was a risk everyone wanted to avoid. Many people were taken to prison just for their political views and those who were viewed as a threat to the government were taken from their homes and never heard from again. Many families learned years later about the fate of their loved ones taken by the government. Most of them had been executed. Our secretive exit from Kabul included a short goodbye with our immediate family including grandparents, aunts, and uncles. Even they were sworn the secrecy by my parents to not mention anything about our intention to escape Afghanistan until we were completely out of the country.

We worried about travelling as a family with young children through the dangerous mountain passes between Kabul and Pakistan. Some of the fiercest fighting between the Soviets and the rebel forces took place in the part of Afghanistan we were about to travel through. Our loved ones had worries of their own, such as the increase in rockets attacks on Kabul and their chances for survival. As we left our family behind, we had to leave part of our hearts with them. I think that part of us will always remain there, given that we knew our chances of seeing each other again in this lifetime was unlikely.

## War children grow up fast

At the age of fifteen, I was deemed old enough to be trusted with taking care of my family. This did not come to me as a surprise, because my father could not leave as quickly as we did. Dad had to stay behind to finalize our affairs in Kabul, given that we had no intention of ever returning. So, I was trusted with the responsibility of taking my mother, two sisters, and brother out of the country. Thankfully, I was about to do this with the help of a trusted relative and someone whom I had never met before as our guide, who I got to know very well. At the time, I never thought of how heavy this responsibility was, I just accepted it as something I had to do. Years later, as life became normal again, I realized that at the age of fifteen, a boy should be focused on what type of sports to play, having a social circle, focusing on his studies, and maybe chasing after girls. As a parent I could not imagine my children going through what I did as a teenager.

"Here is ten thousand dollars (thirty years ago, ten thousand dollars was the equivalent of about fifty thousand or so in Canada at the time of writing) and you are now responsible to safely take your mom, sisters, and brother out of the country. Don't ever lose sight of them and don't lose the money. When you get to Pakistan, find a safe apartment, buy only the necessities of life and always stay at home to make sure everyone is okay." These words were spoken to me by my father only once and yet, tattooed onto my brain. How was I to fulfill this important responsibility? I did not know. But I had faith and I knew that no matter what, I had to be brave and carry on. In my mind, this was the time in my life that I had to become a warrior and knew that this characteristic would stay with me for the rest of my life.

I began to visualize my new role in life. Yes, I was only fifteen years old, I never had to protect my family, nor had I ever held or fired a gun before, but I knew that no matter what laid ahead, I could do all these things. After all, this was about protecting our honour. The Afghan people hold honour above all and sacrificing everything, including one's life, to defend their honour was a given. This was no different for me.

As we prepared to leave Kabul, I no longer thought of myself as a fifteen-year-old kid who could go to dad for help. The responsibility of figure things out on behalf of my dad was now mine. In 1989, when venturing into the countryside in Afghanistan, especially outside of Kabul, was to venture into a man's world. Women rarely dealt with matters such as the journey we were about to take. So, I had to speak up and take charge. Despite this cultural reality, having a high level of respect for women was taught to me by everyone as part of my formative years, so I never did anything without input from my mom during our journey out of Afghanistan. In our home, mom and dad were equally respected, responsible, and in charge of our life decisions.

As a family who lived in Kabul for many generations, it was a tremendous change for us to leave city life. For the first time in our lives, we were about to experience what the rest of Afghanistan was like. Although my mom had travelled to several parts of the country during times of peace for family trips, this trip was much different. Women in Kabul dressed liberally, and it was rare to see a woman covered from head to toe. For my mother and sister, this was quite a change they had to make for the sake of safely escaping the country. They had to prepare themselves by looking the part of Afghan women from the villages. The traditional head to toe dress, referred to as a burka, which women used to wear about a century ago was the safest outfit for an Afghan woman when travelling out of Kabul.

I remember my mother and sister fitting their burkas. They were struggling to see through the tiny holes in front of their faces. They could barely walk straight, and it often looked like they would trip or fall. It was difficult to breathe in this attire, but they had to wear it. Most of the world had no idea what the burka was until footage from Afghanistan came to light in 2001. The stories of brutality by extremists who made women wear this outfit all over Afghanistan to abide by their radical beliefs created a better sense of understanding about the oppression of women in Afghanistan during that time. Those who didn't abide by them were punished for violating their rules. For women who were raised and lived in Kabul, their faces spoke volumes about how such practices was sending the Afghan women back to the dark ages. Women's rights in Afghanistan had made progress for many decades before the war but they were sent back about a century during and after the war.

I knew that we had to be prepared and would travel through some of the toughest terrain in Afghanistan. Most of these areas in southern Afghanistan had suffered from Soviet bombings and the fighting between the Soviets and the rebel fighters. Most villages were left in desperate conditions with no electricity, running water, hospitals, or even roads. Despite the country being in a state of war, which deprived those living in Kabul from electricity during blackouts, we still had the luxury of running water, hospitals, and other necessities of life.

The areas we were about to travel through were controlled by the rebel fighters. Rebels were feared by many and used the mountains of Afghanistan, which they knew so well, to their advantage. They had kept the Soviet troops out of these areas for almost a decade. Despite all that I knew about the rebels, I wasn't afraid of them. I thought that they were Afghans just like me, they spoke the same language as we did, and shared the same basic cultural values. At that time, I only saw the rebels as braver and caring more than I about their country than those who were trying to flee. I related to them because I respected their love of the country and their willingness to lose their lives defending it. In a way, I was fond of the rebels, they bravely fought the Soviets with very basic means and eventually drove them out. I thought that they were the true freedom fighters. I was excited to meet the rebels, speak with them, and get to know them better.

The ability to adapt quickly and blend into the villages of Afghanistan despite being a city kid came easily. I think it was because fear and lack of confidence were not optional. I knew that we were taking this trip to save our lives, and I matured very quickly. I also knew that this was the biggest challenge of my life, and anything that life threw at me after this was not likely going to intimidate or change me very much.

Escaping a war zone and living to talk about it is one of the biggest challenges a human being can face. It makes life's other challenges and goals trivial after a person experiences such an ordeal. This mentality was cemented in my mind for the rest of my life and proved to be a major source of strength for me as a person and in my work as a police officer about a decade later. Going into a crack house, a gang hangout, or into a gun fight during police training and the uncertainties that came with them never intimidated me. This is probably why I frustrated my instructors during the police undercover training course. It seemed like nothing that they threw at me ever scared or excited me. For an undercover police officer, this was not a good trait to have. Undercover police officers always need to be on edge to stay safe in dangerous places.

As we prepared to depart for our journey out of Afghanistan and I began to embrace a new way of dressing, thinking, and carrying myself, I also started to meet some of the toughest people in the world. They were the Afghan villagers and rebel fighters. Their mental strength amazed me as I began to learn more about them. Their selflessness and dedication to drive out the Soviets out of Afghanistan at any cost, combined with their strong belief in their faith, eventually made them unstoppable. One such person was our guide. He welcomed our family to his humble home just outside of Kabul. At first sight, my immaturity and judgemental thoughts took over; looking at a middle-aged man who was walking on crutches, missing one leg, and speaking in a simple language worried me. Is this the guy we must rely on to safely get us out of a war zone? How can he help us? Can he even take care of himself?

Within a day of staying in our guide's family home prior to our departure, I learned about this man and his life. Photographs of him, and the other men in his family, told me part of the story and he started to complete the rest while joking with us about the days where he had both of his legs. I learned that this man was a former rebel fighter. He had been in many firefights with the Soviet troops and had killed some of them. He and most of the men in his family had been rebel fighters. The man looked proud while telling us the story, which I still vividly remember. He always began by putting in his mouth a small amount of what is know in Afghanistan as Naswar. This is similar to chewing tobacco. Once he had put the Naswar in his mouth, he would sound a bit odd, yet this made his story telling even more interesting. All I had to do was to ask one question and he began the story.

Me:       So, uncle Dauod, what was it like getting
          into a firefight with the Soviets?

He always started his sentences with Wallah, which
means "by God".

Dauod:  Wallah, on that day, we had the clearest view
          of the dirt road. Mostly because we found a
          new spot on the side of a mountain which
          gave us enough protection from being shot
          at from the road, but it was also safe from
          airstrikes by the Soviet planes, so we knew
          that if a convoy drove through that day, we
          would attack them.

          We got to our sangar (place to set up for an
          attack), right after morning prayer. So, the
          darkness had just started to fade away and
          we could see where we were going. All ten
          of us lugged our gear, including the rockets
          we were going to set up to take out the tanks.
          Then, with our binoculars, we sat there all
          morning and no convoy in sight. Then, just
          past noon, we heard the rumbling of the
          tanks; this was our lucky day. We were set
          up and ready to take out the convoy. But
          despite agreeing that we would take out the
          end of the convoy so that the other tanks
          could not turn around to fire back at us,
          one of the young guys started to fire at the
          Soviets as soon as he saw the first tank.

Now we were in a terrible position. With the first tank taken out, we started to take fire from the rest of the tanks and some of the Soviet soldiers started to hit the ground and look around for us. Luckily, we were high up and had the advantage. We fired all our rockets and disabled half of the convoy, then took out the soldiers with machine gun fire. Some of the guys scattered to shoot the Soviets who were on the ground and stop them from climbing up and firing at us. This is where I saw some of our guys drop. I knew that some of us would be killed for sure on that day.

About four hours went by, and we played a game of hide and seek with the Soviets many times by not firing at them at all for a while just to see if they would think we are all dead and get back on their tanks and leave. But the Soviets tried the same thing. Eventually the firefight started again; as we saw some of the Soviets walking back to their tanks, we shot at them. It was near the end where we almost killed half of the Soviets and disabled most of their tanks that they decided to run away. I got up to fire at the last two tanks which were about to take off as the Soviets fired back and shot me.

Me:     Is this where you lost your leg?

Daoud: Wallah, my leg is a whole different story. On the day we killed all those Soviets, they only shot me on the side of the abdomen, and I healed from that within weeks. Here, look at the scar (he lifts of his shirt to show the left side of his lower abdomen). This was not enough to stop me.

When it was all over, I realized that my brother and son had been killed. Several others were wounded. It was dark by the time we stumbled down the mountain with all of our gear and came down to the village. I was too weak to go up again, but we sent a group of men to go back up the mountain and bring down our shaheedan (those who lose their life to protect their honour).

Me: So, what happened to your leg then? Another firefight with the Soviets?

Daoud: Wallah, this was just when I was walking.

Me: Walking? How can that be?

Daoud: Wallah, I always thought that I would be killed or lose a limb in a firefight with the Soviets, but not while walking just outside of my village. I stepped on a landmine in a field and it exploded. After the dust settled, even though I thought the mine blew me up to pieces, I realized that the only thing

I could no longer feel was my leg and that blood was gushing out of my thigh. I knew that with a severed leg, lying there was going to be a sure death, so I started to drag myself. I dragged myself on my chest for what seemed to take forever until I reached the first gravel road then I could see a fellow villager who picked me up.

This was the first time I met someone who was the victim of the millions of land mines buried by the Soviet troops all over Afghanistan. The land mines had created hundreds of thousands of amputees all over the country. This was the same for our guide.

As I listened to his story, I thought to myself that if he was an example of how all the rebel fighters carried themselves, then the Soviets had no chance of ever winning the war against the Afghan rebels. It sounded to me that his biggest disappointment was not because he lost a leg, but that he could no longer go back to battle. Despite all their advanced weapons and being one of the world's superpowers at the time, the passion and selflessness of the rebels was what gave me hope that Soviets would be on their way out of Afghanistan one day. Our guide told us that his passion for still doing something to help his people made him became a guide who could help families escape the war. As I got to know this man over the next week or so of travelling out of Afghanistan, I saw the incredible physical and mental toughness in him.

Travelling with a family including women and young children across southern Afghanistan limited our ability to carry things. We had to travel by foot, truck, or any other mode of transportation that was available—our allowance to pack was limited only to what we could carry. So, we literally left with almost nothing more than the clothes on our backs. We were assured by our guide that, as we passed through the small villages in southern Afghanistan, we would meet some of the poorest people in the world; however, they were also some of the most generous people in the world. We were assured that no matter what, we would be the guest of the villagers at nights and for every meal. Our guide was truly amazing. He had taken this journey many times and had built lasting relationships with many people in the small villages we were about to pass. We benefited from his ability to build trusting relationships with others during a time where we did not know anyone to go to for help. We were welcomed by Afghans in the small villages who knew that we were from Kabul and had left everyone and everything behind to escape the country. I was pessimistic about being greeted warmly by Afghans in remote villages. I thought that they may not care for us city folks passing through their villages and leaving them behind. And yet, during our travels through the snow filled winter wonderland and cold temperatures, our fellow Afghans surprised me with their kindness. They saved us from hunger and sheltered us from the cold in their humble homes. We travelled through villages surrounded by some of the most beautiful mountains in the world. The snow-covered mountains almost burned my eyes when I looked at them, and the bitter cold seemed much more than what we were used to in the city of Kabul.

For the first portion of our trip, we boarded an old bus. I was told that, as we travelled through southern Afghanistan, the rebel-controlled areas were of no concern; however, there were pockets where the Soviet troops were still in control of the area. The Soviets had set up checkpoints to prevent young men from escaping the country. Should they find me, I would be detained and drafted into the army. I had to hide from the Soviets before approaching these checkpoints. I had no idea where to hide but I put my faith in the hands of our guide and the bus driver who had taken this trip on many occasions. Prior to reaching these checkpoints, the bus would stop on the side of the road in a quiet area surrounded by mountains. I was asked to leave the bus and the driver would take me to my hiding place. The driver would open the rear panel of the bus where the engine block was located and pointed to a compartment just big enough for me to squeeze into. I was told to face the outside, so I could breathe through the tiny holes, to be quiet—especially anytime the bus stopped—and tuck my arms onto my chest so as to not touch something in the engine block or the belts and lose my fingers or hands.

I quickly learned to follow these directions. For the next hour or so, I was squeezed into that box like a human pretzel, but I got through it. I made my body as small as I could by squeezing all my limbs close to my body, then tucked my head in between my legs while seated. As the blood circulation started to decrease to my limbs, I felt my legs going numb. It is these types of moments that allows a person to seek strength and endurance from within. As difficult as this was, I believe that this taught me an important lesson in life. As humans, we can endure extreme difficultly and face fear if we look to the self. I learned that God or the higher power is inside of us, and not something that we need to search for. At one checkpoint, I heard the angry voices of Soviet soldiers. By this time, I had learned a few Russian words and I knew that they were demanding something from the bus driver.

I had heard that Soviets were sometimes irate and would empty their rifles into the compartments of a vehicle if they suspected that someone might be hiding in it. As I sat there beside the old and noisy engine, I could not hear much but as the voices came closer, I saw the green wool uniform and black boots of a Soviet soldier. I also saw the bayonet at the tip of his rifle. As I peeked through the small holes inches away from my face, I saw that there was not just one but three Soviet soldiers each holding their hands out for a share of a bribe. The bus driver calmly took the money out of his pocket and divided it between them. At that time, I was not familiar with things like infringing on a person's freedom of movement, unlawful detention, bribery, and corruption, but I knew intuitively that this was wrong. After we passed this checkpoint the bus pulled over some distance away and I was taken out of the compartment and sat back inside the bus.

As I sat in the bus and looked at the fields surrounded by snow covered mountains and the odd small house which stood isolated inside the small Afghan villages we were passing, I understood why the Afghan people were rising against the Soviets. I began to comprehend that when humans are held hostages in their own homeland, they want to free themselves. I understood the hate of the Afghan people for the Soviet soldiers even more. Today, I appreciate the fundamental human rights and freedoms I and other Canadians enjoy under our Charter of Rights and Freedoms and have defended these rights for many years as a Canadian police officer. This appreciation for human rights began when I was fifteen and inhaling diesel fuel in the hidden compartment of a bus trying to escape a war-torn Afghanistan.

As we entered the rebel-controlled areas, I was relieved. I trusted our guide who knew what was ahead in this journey. Given that our guide could only hold his crutches and talk to people, he thought it was necessary for me to shoulder a rifle as we moved through parts of the rebel-controlled villages—just in case something happened. My role was to pretend that I was a young rebel fighter. This was way more exciting than hiding in a box beside a bus engine, and I welcomed the role. Handing me an AK rifle and showing how to aim it, where the trigger was, and how to change the magazines was my first introduction to guns and my first training in firearms. Now that I think about being introduced to a rifle at the age of fifteen, it reminds me that I was forced at a very early age to grow up fast.

Holding a machine gun and walking through villages in southern Afghanistan with my family, dressed like villagers, made me feel as if I were indeed a rebel fighter. The possibility of having to aim the gun and shoot at a person was far from my mind. But I knew that kids just like me were shooting at the Soviets. After carrying this rifle for a while, the novelty wore off, and I thought about all the evil these guns had caused in Afghanistan and the many innocent lives lost because of the abundance of guns in my homeland. For the remainder of the journey, I just couldn't wait to get to a point where I could hand over the gun back and never have to hold one again.

As we moved deeper into southern Afghanistan, I realized how difficult life was for people who lived outside of Kabul. I saw many young boys around my age who were rebel fighters. While I was merely playing the role of a rebel fighter for a few days, their faces were tough, their youthful and innocent looks a thing of the past as they walked shoulder to shoulder with other rebel fighters. It was not until much later that I learned about child soldiers not only in Afghanistan, but around the world. As I researched this more later in life, I learned that young boys like those I saw in Afghanistan were being used in many war-torn places to further political agendas that they often knew nothing about. It was after this experience that my perspective changed about humans and the chances we are given in life. I learned that despite what I was going through, others who were just like me had it much worse. I knew that many young Afghan boys would likely never see anything outside of their villages, have a chance to obtain an education, enjoy a life of peace and prosperity, and have an opportunity to flourish to their full potential.

It took us four days to pass through the villages and mountains of southern Afghanistan. Time went by very quickly because we were continuously on the move, but it also felt like I saw and experienced a lifetime of new things. The scenic mountains of Afghanistan, the lives of those who lived in the valleys surrounded by such tough and at times inaccessible terrain, their perseverance to survive harsh winters while having access to the very basic necessities of life, all of it amazed me. A sense of sadness accompanied my amazement, as I knew that it was unlikely for life to improve for those whose fate in life was to endure the difficulties most others in the world could only read about or see in a documentary. At that time, I was still far away from the luxuries of life in North America, yet even comparing the life we had in Kabul seemed much easier than the life experienced by those living in small Afghan villages. The added threat of violence brought on by war made life truly difficult for them, but somehow, they kept going.

## Our life as refugees - lessons in compassion

Nearing the border with Pakistan was a shock to all of us. Up to this point, we were Afghans travelling inside our country. No matter who we met, people had been easy to speak with and we shared a collective understanding. This was about to end abruptly as we crossed the southern border into Pakistan. When I hear people talk about how similar Afghanistan is to Pakistan, I know that they have a limited idea of what they are talking about. Assumptions about the similarity in culture and way of life between these two countries are mostly based on historic views from western societies who never understood this part of the world. For Afghans like us who lived our lives in a city, it was a complete culture shock.

One of my first experiences in Pakistan was at the border, where police openly asked for a bribe for each person entering their country. This was money that went directly into the pockets of border guards who would turn anyone away if they didn't pay. After paying them, we could cross into their country. Our guide told me that this is how it goes in Pakistan—for some things you need to pay officials, so have the money ready to pay or you will have difficulties. I tried not to let this totally skew my impression of Pakistan; yes, it was disappointing, but at least we were safe. I also learned that just because humans are suffering, it doesn't mean others always respond with kindness and compassion. Although we experienced acts of kindness from the Pakistanis, we were still in a foreign land and could tell the stark difference between living in Kabul and where we were.

Thanks to the hard work of my father, we had enough funds to keep us out of the refugee camps while living in Pakistan. These camps were tents in the middle of the desert and millions of Afghan refugees lived in these camps for many years as the war went on. Typically, the tents were made of some type of cloth and held up by wooden sticks. They were frail and could easily be destroyed if a storm or even heavy wind blew through them. Families with their children would make these tents into a home just to survive another night. They had to walk far to get clean water, food, and other basic necessities. This is a life which is difficult to describe, this is one of those things that can only be fully understood if a person actually sees these camps, hears the sounds and smells the scents to appreciate what some humans call home.

As we settled into a very small apartment, with five of us sleeping in the same room, we considered ourselves luckier than most. Our apartment was basically one large room with a bathroom on the one end and a small kitchen on the other. The kitchen was basically a small room with a burner on the ground and one shelf to put a few dishes on. I would come across the Afghan refugees who sometimes left the camps just to venture out. Looking at them alone was enough to know that their life in the refugee camps was unbearable for most of them. The heat in this part of the world combined with the humidity and unsanitary conditions created a very difficult life for Afghan refugees. I often thought about them on very hot days, when being indoors and having access to a fan made the heat barely tolerable. I knew that many Afghan refugees gave birth, got sick, struggled to find food, or died. I was grateful for what we had even though it was far worse than our life in Kabul. Our sanctuary was that one single room—there, we were free of oppression, especially the women in my family. Afghan women were expected to be covered from head to toe, not speak with anyone, not laugh in public, and not go anywhere alone. It was extremely difficult for my mother and sisters to accept this new reality. I would describe the life of those who lived inside the refugee camps in Pakistan the same as life in prison. They had no rights or freedoms and were bound by many restrictions. In places like this, people are lucky if their basic human rights are respected, let alone all the other things that people around the world take for granted.

Until my father arrived several months later, I took on his role by doing as much as I could so that no one from my family would have to interact with the people outside. I disliked being in Pakistan, but it gave me the ability to endure uncertainty yet keep a positive outlook on life. I looked at all of this as a test of our character, a rite of passage of sorts. I decided that no matter where I ended up, I would remain a compassionate person and would work in an area where I can help others. It is why I later became a police officer in Canada.

During one sweltering summer day in Pakistan, I was walking to get the day's groceries. I was drenched in sweat after five minutes due to the muggy air combined with the heat. I suddenly heard gunfire. This caught me by surprise, because I thought the sound of gunshots were likely no longer part of our lives. I tried not to panic as the gunfire was not close and it was only one short burst. However, I still wondered about what took place because I associated gunfire with death and destruction. I knew that the direction of the gunfire was near the market I visited every morning to get our basic food items for the day. I was hesitant to go but had no choice. We needed our groceries, so I let some time go by then started to walk to the market. On the way there, I thought about possible scenarios. What could have happened? Would I see another dead person? I arrived at the market and noticed that someone had been killed in public. A chaotic scene was still unfolding as onlookers had surrounded the dead man's body. I was surprised that the police had not taken the man's body away after all this time. I had no desire to get close to the body, but I could see that his blood had spattered onto the nearby wall where he had collapsed. More sadness filled my heart and I did my best to cope with it prior to walking back home. Later I learned that this was the execution of a prominent Afghan writer who was killed for expressing his views about rebel leaders and criticizing them. This slowly became the norm as various rebel groups started to fight each other. Eventually these disputes carried into Afghanistan, leading to a civil war and creating a fertile ground for extremists. The non-Afghan terrorists took advantage of this and came to Afghanistan to train and organize prior to launching the terror attacks on the US in September 2001.

As we continued our lives in Pakistan, I also tried to look at Afghan refugees from the eyes of the people of Pakistan. The Afghan rebels presented themselves as an intimidating force. They often walked freely on the streets of Pakistan and were heavily armed with machine guns. The trucks they drove were often armoured SUVs and they did not seem to care or respect any of the rules in Pakistan. I could see the look of frustration on the face of Pakistani police as they watched the heavily armed Afghan rebels drive around in their cities while the Pakistani police officers were walking on foot holding a stick in their hand as their only weapon.

The violence, such as political executions of Afghans by their rivals, added another level of intimidation and threat to the lives of Pakistani people. This made me look at the people of Pakistan with sympathy, and I tried to understand their frustrations and realized that they were likely overwhelmed with the Afghan refugee crisis. I tried very hard to understand many things, but was still disappointed about the lack of integrity and the lack of a system that could account for the billions of dollars in aid from countries around the world destined for the Afghan refugees. Much of the funds were stolen by those who were in power because of corruption and the refugees continued to suffer in silence.

The one year we spent in Pakistan seemed like a lifetime. However, I continued to keep things into perspective by thinking about those Afghan refugees who had left during the early years of war and were still living in tents for many years; they had a much more difficult life. Our plan was to leave this country as soon as possible and establish a life in a peaceful and prosperous country. This was an unattainable dream for most of the Afghan refugees. Most of them had no ability or the means to do anything about their living conditions. They could only wait for the war to be over so that one day, they may return to what was left of their homeland.

My father joined us in Pakistan a few months later. Our whole family was excited because we were all back together. Our dream of moving on with our life to a better place seemed closer. Our parents were easy going with a good sense of humour, which kept us going while living in Pakistan. They were skilfully taking most of our worries away by attempting to create the best family environment they could for us under the circumstances. We no longer had a house, no relatives to visit us, no chance for an education or employment and were mostly bound to our one room apartment in a country which we could not wait to get out of. With all this happening, we still cherished our time together and often talked about our life and family in Kabul. We counted ourselves lucky to have a chance at a safer life soon.

We were unable to attend school, but my father brought us books and taught us basic English in preparation for our eventual immigration to Canada. Dad believed that no matter which part of the world a person ends up in, it is her or his duty to learn the language and understand the laws and culture of that part of the world. Dad looked at this as a sign of respect for our fellow humans. He said that trying to learn about others and speaking their language not only makes us a better person, it also removes obstacles.

My parents' selfless and risky decision to leave their homeland with four young children, live in a strange country, and endure uncertainty in search of a new life cemented an important value for me. This value was to take risks and not be a coward. I used their example and carried these values with me by thinking of others before thinking of myself and taking risks where most people would dare not. Almost two decades later, in my role as a police leader, I took many risks while standing up for others, even if sometimes, taking these risks resulted in my being attacked. However, I placed minimal value in these setbacks because I was doing the right thing for the right reason and never was afraid of reprisal.

Our last few weeks in Pakistan were a blur. Once we received the news from Canadian immigration officials that our family was accepted to immigrate to Canada, the days could not go by fast enough. Having lived a life of uncertainty for over a year, we were all excited to leave for Canada no matter what it would be like. All we knew was that life would restart for us and that we would have a second chance at a future and a place to call home. As we prepared to leave, my heart went out to the millions of Afghans who were either left behind with no promise of a future or fell victim to the atrocities of war. I was overcome with a sense of guilt that we were leaving for a better life but tried to be grateful for the opportunity that our family was lucky enough to escape this life.

During my life as a police officer in Canada, I met many Canadians in various prisons across the country, and my life as a refugee enabled me to relate to them easily. I looked at them through a lens similar as those who were stuck in refugee camps in Pakistan, where they had to endure being in a place without much hope. The only thing to look forward to was for the days to pass by quickly enough so that they could one day get out. I knew that being in an unpleasant place, especially against your will, would make any human appreciate the values of freedom and peace. I often felt that our time as refugees was sort of like being in prison. We were safe but did not have the same rights, opportunities, and freedoms as everyone else. Time stood still for us and we had no choice but to wait and do our time until we were able to live life again. There is an old and beautiful Farsi poem by an Afghan named Abul Qasem Lahouti—which later became a well-known song by the late Ahmad Zahir, a beloved Afghan artist—that says: "Life will eventually end, there is no need for submission. If submission were a must, then there is no need for living." I certainly related to this poem during our time as refugee. I know the value of freedom.

## Life free of war

In my life as a Canadian, I have heard on many occasions the discontent of those who are less than thrilled with having to pay so much taxes. Their hard-earned income is often slashed substantially after they have paid their dues to the tax man, leaving them with less to take care of themselves and their families. I have always empathized with their reactions as they vent about paying too much taxes. However, I often remind them of all the good their taxes do in Canada and elsewhere in the world. I use my life and our family's immigration to Canada as examples of how the average Canadian taxpayer helped humanity. As a refugee family who had neither the ability nor means to make our way into Canada on our own, we were in need. Canadian taxpayers' money helps us start a new life. So, over the past three decades, I have gladly contributed as a taxpayer, knowing that some of it helps others. The unfortunate people who face obstacles in life due to war, just like we did, need these contributions.

Our first day of true freedom after a year-long life of uncertainty was a crisp and cold October day in 1990 when we landed at Toronto's Pearson Airport. Arriving in Canada after the experience we had gone through was one of the high points in our family's life. My parents looked relieved. They knew that no matter what our future held, it included safety and a country to call home. After a long and difficult flight across the seas, our next short trip from Toronto to our destination, Winnipeg, was very pleasant. For the next year, the kind people of Manitoba truly lived up to their province's nickname, Friendly Manitoba. Winnipeg's frosty winter was about to start, and the freezing temperatures made for some truly Canadian winter days. We walked everywhere and used public transit to acquaint ourselves with our new city.

Despite the freezing weather, our hearts were warm and content in Winnipeg. We were no longer in limbo. The excitement of entering our first apartment in Canada, enrolling in school and purchasing necessities were all good signs of starting a new life in a great country. My parents reminded us to be grateful during our first family dinner in Canada. My parents also reminded us to try our best, be a lifelong learner, live an honest life, and make the best of every situation and opportunity. Initially, I wondered if Canada would truly welcome us and allow for us to flourish. But in Winnipeg, we only experienced kindness and compassion.

On our first day of high school in Winnipeg, the school principal met with us and welcomed us to the school and to Canada. Without speaking much English, we tried our best to absorb the information and communicate with everyone. On our second day of school, our principal checked in on us again. My sister and I both seemed a bit worried about our transition and not being able to speak much English. We told the principal that we thought we were not fitting in and we had some worries about our upcoming struggles in a new country. The school principal did something that day that left an indelible positive impression on us. He walked us outside to the front of the school and showed us a sign on the old announcement board. In those days, school messages were posted on plastic boards on which letters slid in to form words. The sign read 'Welcome Bari and Massoudah from Afghanistan.' The school had honoured our heritage and welcomed us. I thought about this announcement board often and to this day, think that these types of gestures, however small, make immigrants strive to become the best they can be. It motivates them to contribute to the richness of the country because they feel welcomed and included.

I knew that nice gestures and acts of kindness by Canadians was not the only thing that would help us succeed or establish our life as new immigrants. However, it was reassuring that society, for the most part, was full of people who welcomed us. I felt like this about Canada and the US for many years until the divisive politics of 2016 in the US and other countries brought to the surface the hidden racism and discrimination against immigrants. In 2016, I looked back almost thirty years and felt that for some reason, such attitudes towards immigrants was rare during the time we were new immigrants. The fear of immigrants had either increased significantly or was just being brought to surface at this time. Either way, I was disappointed by the backwards movement in this area. Self-discipline and perseverance were two key guiding principles for me as an immigrant kid that helped me integrate.

My initial goal in Canada was to complete high school. I played soccer in our high school team and enjoyed the support of my teachers and teammates. Even though I was never a strong soccer player, I still felt great about having the opportunity to partake in a team sport. This is something that my father and other generations whose childhood was not tainted by war had experienced. I felt that, in my new life, I got to see some normalcy as a high school kid, which gave me the added encouragement and motivation to embrace life in Canada. I started to feel a sense of normalcy after several months of being in Canada. Delivering the Winnipeg Free Press newspaper was my first job. Riding a bicycle in the snow was a challenge, but I loved having a job and wanted to be productive. As a first-generation immigrant, I knew that, to be successful, I had to work hard and do well. This mindset became part of my life later as a Canadian—even after being well established.

As we settled into our first truly Canadian winter in Winnipeg, the joys of exploring the city continued. The minus thirty-degree temperature at the corner of Portage and Main, with its world-famous wind chill factor, gave me a taste of what it was like to be a real Canadian. It was a joy because the winter wonderland in a safe and prosperous country was better compared to worrying about who might shoot at me. I could not hear explosions and knew that the worst that could happen might be frostbite. I always thought to myself what a difference peace and security make for the human mind. For me it was a privilege to live such a peaceful life and I know that, for those who have seen nothing but peace all their life, these things can more easily be taken for granted.

In 1991, our family moved to British Columbia. We experienced many wonderful interactions with Canadians at all levels during our first year while living in Winnipeg. So, I guess it was time to experience some ignorance and discrimination. Our first visit with an immigration official in Vancouver was less than pleasant. The lady who spoke with us seemed to be unhappy in general and fed up with immigrants coming to BC from other parts of Canada. She made it clear to us that we should have stayed in Winnipeg as BC had, in her opinion, too many immigrants already.

My father's ability to communicate in English flawlessly and his knowledge of the Canadian Charter of Right and Freedoms stunned the official.

Dad was quick to stand up for our rights, something we all learned from him. He taught us that, to be able to demand your rights, you must first educate yourself. I thought Dad was about to start by telling the official that he was not about to take her abuse, that he had lived in Manhattan for twenty years and knew all that there was to know about his rights, so how dare she speak with him like that. I'm sure he was feeling all those things, but Dad kept his calm. He had familiarized himself enough with the Canadian Charter of Rights once we arrived in Canada to know what his rights were. Dad's response to the unwelcoming comments by the immigration official was a quote from the Charter, delivered with a smile on his face. I learned much later that this was the section called Freedom of Mobility. It was many years later that I started to understand the power and complexities of the Canadian Charter of Rights and Freedoms. I learned the importance of the Charter during my work as a police investigator. I saw how skilful defense lawyers critically examined and picked apart our work during criminal trials, when any violation of a person's rights was taken very seriously by the courts. But even without a law degree or courtroom skills, Dad made an effective Charter argument.

Dad's comments did not make the immigration official any happier. However, it silenced her, because she knew that there was nothing she could do to prevent us from moving anywhere we wanted. I sat there silently and looked at my family. Everyone seemed disappointed by our interactions with this person. After that meeting, I knew that fully learning and understanding the Charter was my first task prior to becoming a Canadian. That night, Dad told us that, when speaking to people such as the unpleasant immigration official, a gentle tone and respectful demeanour were the only way to accomplish our objectives. Dad emphasized that although obnoxious behaviour such as yelling or physical violence was something lots of people resort to all over the world, it is not a civil way to solve anything. Since that day, I never once had a physical confrontation with anyone in Canada in my personal life. Ironically, years later, I found myself as a Canadian police officer who had to use physical force on many occasions to control others who were acting violently.

## Things about my birthplace I never miss

The ability for a person to be able to defend their basic human rights in a free and democratic society is something I and many other immigrants never take for granted. Being in Canada and having the protection of the laws supporting human rights and individual freedoms reminded me of the lack thereof in other parts of the world. I remember how, as a child, the human suffering because of war in Afghanistan was at the forefront of my mind because it concerned personal safety and took away our peace and security. It wasn't until many years later that other injustices against the Afghans at the hands of their own became as disturbing to me as wounds of war.

The persecution of certain people in Afghanistan due to ethnicity, religion, or socio-economic status started to bother me a great deal. As I continued to live in Canada and learned about the fundamental individual rights, it became more evident to me that most countries still struggle with providing such rights to their people. Both subtle and systematic discrimination—even in progressive countries such as Canada—have existed for many years. The treatment of the Indigenous people has improved only to a certain degree over the last one hundred years in Canada. It is obvious that Canada has much more work to do in creating an equal and inclusive society. Despite all this, it was easier for me to understand such inequalities in Canada, because so many demographic changes occurred in such a brief time. The stark differences between European settlers, Indigenous, and those from other ethnicities who later immigrated to Canada would obviously create conflict. And this conflict would take some time to resolve. Yes, people had to struggle to be heard, but at least someone listened to them and progress was being made. I had a very difficult time understanding why such progress was not being made in my birthplace. The way people treated those who were less fortunate than them disturbed me and unfortunately, I saw this both as a child in Afghanistan and later as a Canadian police officer during my interactions with some immigrants in Canada who stubbornly held on to their old ways.

In the old part of Kabul, where the merchants opened their shops before daybreak, there was a market called Mandawi, which was basically a row of stores on each side of the street selling essential food items. Rice, beans, flour, and herbs and spices were lined up in front of the stores in large bags. There was no price attached to them and depending on how much a person wanted to buy, one could negotiate the price with the merchants. People purchased anywhere from a few to some fifty kilograms of rice or four. The closest thing that resembles such markets are some stores in places like Chinatowns in major North American cities. Those who could afford it would visit Mandawi and, depending on how much money they had, they would buy their choice items ranging from the cheapest available to the best quality. I was introduced to Mandawi by my father who would take me there every few months to purchase our bulk items. The biggest purchases were always made just before winter as the leaves changed colour and the crisp Kabul fall season fell upon the city. Most families would take this opportunity to stock up on the most needed items for their winter cooking needs, rice and flour being the most popular items.

Carrying the heavy rice and flour bags around was almost exclusively the job of fellow Afghans from outside Kabul. These men were deprived of an education, opportunities, and a chance to do anything else but continue this job generation after generation. They were called Jowalees. Just by looking at these men you would be deceived about the incredible strength they possessed. Most of them looked old and frail. Their ability to lift the heavy bags of rice and flour weighing more than one hundred pound and loading them onto their backs was an act of incredible physical strength. However, I was mostly amazed at their mental toughness. I respected the work these men did and at the same time wondered about their thoughts on having to be serving the needs of others who sometimes were just terrible people.

One day, Dad and I were asking for help to carry the things we had purchased, and Dad always treated everyone with respect. I was not accustomed to a person speaking in a demeaning way to those whose help we relied on. I spotted a burly man, his gut popping out in front of him, a typical over-consumer of food in Afghanistan. During a time where most of the country had little to no means of feeding their families, being overly big was rare. The chubby man was yelling at one of the Jowalees. As I watched, the Jowalee, who was an old man, moved slowly as he had two heavy bags of rice on his back, the weight of it bending him in half. The chubby man was not only yelling at the Jowalee, he was also pushing him to move faster. The old man's response to this was: "Yes, sir." As the chubby man became more frustrated, he took the headdress off the Jowalee, threw it on the ground and called him useless. In Afghan culture, it is insulting and demeaning to throw a person's headdress to the ground. The Jowalee stopped for a second, picked up his headdress, and said sorry before continuing to walk while being crushed under the heavy weight of the bags.

I was a child and couldn't do anything but watch and feel shame. How could this be? Why didn't the old man fight for his right as a human and ask to be treated with dignity? The only thing I could think of was that, if I were bigger and stronger, I would step in do something. I think this anger took over just because I could not believe that a person would give themselves the right to treat a poor old man this way. The worst part of this was that no one did anything about it.

As I asked myself these questions, I felt a sense of sadness and helplessness. Sadness because mistreating other humans who had no voice was accepted, and helplessness because there was no such thing such as a charter of rights for the people. The lack of a system that can allow those who were less fortunate the ability to be heard angered me. Years later, I thought about this situation and compared it to those who are employed by a company and supported by a union. Anything even close to what I saw would be considered as demeaning and abusive in countries where human rights were respected. Even as a child, I knew how broken the system was and the abuse of an old person at the hands of those who were just too arrogant and selfish went on in all corners of all over the world. I also knew that the country and its people longed for justice and fairness.

As I grew older and got further away from Afghanistan, I started to understand the rage of people in such countries, the lack of stability and laws which could protect citizens in a fair way would naturally force humans to react in some way. In the absence of any other way to make their voices heard, violence became the only way. I believe that, when there is an absence of a system that can ensure that human beings are equally respected, rage and revenge will take over. These types of injustices were perhaps the biggest reason for the lack of unity within the people of Afghanistan once the Soviets were defeated. The Afghan people fought each other for almost a decade afterwards, creating a haven for terrorists.

Later in life, I accepted that my convictions about justice and the equal treatment of people regardless of who they were would have likely resulted in getting into constant conflict with others if I still lived in Afghanistan. Given the abundance of guns and how little life was valued at that time, I could have been killed just by trying to stand up for someone else. In my view, the lack of a solid system and a strong government to implement it was a historic failure of past regimes in Afghanistan. So, the story of abuse continued at the hands of one group upon another, depending on who was in power. A few years after we left, the Taliban ruled Afghanistan with brutal force and people feared for their lives, refusing to even leave their homes because they had virtually no human rights. I would have suffocated under their rule.

As an Afghan-born Canadian who has seen and experienced the pain and suffering of the Afghan people, I have often argued that it was our lack of compassion for each other first that caused much of the tragedy in Afghanistan for many years. Yes, the Soviets and other foreign armies who imposed wars on Afghanistan caused the country to spiral down a very dark hole. But the atrocities committed by Afghans against each other I would never accept. So, it is with this that I say to Afghans and other immigrants that we must be humble and respect the reasonable laws of our new homeland, no matter where in the world we have immigrated. All that is afforded to us today as immigrants is worth applauding and embracing, as we never had it where we came from.

## The ungrateful immigrant in Canada

As a police officer, I was called upon many times to assist other police officers and agencies across the country with investigations. The languages I speak and my understanding of Middle Eastern culture were often the reason other police agencies requested my help. It was during such interactions that I became annoyed with the ignorance of some immigrants. Thankfully, these individuals were few and far in between, but I still could not believe the deep-rooted issues that had followed them to Canada. I had hoped that meeting immigrants—especially from troubled countries—would be a joy, mostly because I expected that they would be just as grateful as I was. Despite being in trouble with the law, those who appreciated their newfound freedoms were pleasant to deal with. In many cases, immigrants were mostly ashamed of finding themselves caught in crime and criminality. For the few who didn't, I was the worst police officer they could deal with.

I was called to assist with a routine drug investigation. A woman was bringing illegal drugs into Canada from a foreign country and was concealing them inside what appeared to be legitimate merchandise. I was to help with the interrogation of this person because she was claiming not to speak English. I watched this interview for about an hour until I had enough of the woman trying to lie and manipulate a less experienced police officer by attacking his lack of cultural understanding. She began to educate the police officer about a few things related to her culture and then started to describe herself in a way that started to aggravate me. To use a psychology term, I was being triggered while listening to this person as she began to speak down to the police officer. She started to explain the importance of the class system in her culture and told the officer that she had come from a class of people in her home country who would never speak with someone like him because he was, in her view, below her.

I learned from the investigators that the woman was claiming to be a refugee from another country and had entered Canada to escape persecution. After listening to the woman for a while, I had enough. I was fuming and wanted to barge into the room and tell this woman how ignorant she was about the role of police in a country such as Canada. My second goal was to ask this person why, if she was from such a high class, had she come to Canada and was bringing in drugs? A fellow senior colleague who could clearly see my outrage stopped me from entering the interview room. He knew that, because of my strong convictions about ungrateful and disrespectful immigrants, I would have added nothing of value to the interview. In fact, I would have made the situation worse. At that moment, I realized that I took such negativity coming from immigrants personally and that my negative reactions to my fellow immigrants was far worse than that of someone born and raised in Canada.

The scenario of encountering immigrants who had lost perspective played out in various forms from time to time in my career as a police officer and my reactions were always the same. I knew that my triggers came from seeing the inequality between different classes of people in my birthplace. I also knew that such inequalities exist in many other parts of the world where people believe that they are above or below others. Regardless of where this classism comes from, it has always been wrong in my view.

The passion and principles behind my intolerance of people who see a stark contrast between different classes of people comes from seeing the damage it can cause. I know that such practices can eventually erode an entire country. I hold the notion that no one is above the law. I don't think that the only reason we enjoy our freedoms while living in a democratic society where human rights are respected for the most part is because we have a charter of rights. I feel that the people of Canada who have come here from all corners of the world and have chosen to live by this charter is what holds our freedoms in place. Affording others the same rights as we would want for ourselves makes up the solid foundation for countries such as Canada. This foundation is still in the making for Canada as waves of new immigrants enter the country every year. I know that immigrants will invest in what is good for the country. Most of them will happily abandon the destructive habits such as dividing humans into classes so that we can continue to build an inclusive society.

It is my view that aside from the land itself, a country does not have much to offer anybody. The richness and beauty of any country and the love people have for their homeland comes from the culture that is created by its people. As an immigrant who sees Canada as an example of how to bring the best of the world together, I have often felt blessed that our family ended up here. From the outset, I believed that immigrants like me setting an example of how to live, become educated, work, and interact with others is the only opportunity that we have to show Canadians how valuable we are to this society. I do not think this is about pleasing anyone—the only person I compete with is myself. I knew that, as an immigrant, I would face many struggles; however, my belief in the good of others, and having the mental toughness to persevere through the challenges would eventually lead me to success. Also, I never defined success as being famous, making a certain amount of money, doing a certain type of work or even influencing people. I define success as being able to regrow my roots in a new place after it was ripped out of its original soil. I know that, in their hearts, all immigrants wish they could regrow their roots so that the next generation does not suffer as they did.

# CHAPTER 3

# New Home

## Becoming Canadian

Our life as a new immigrant family was simple. Yet we felt that we lived a life full of amazing experiences. Our family lived in the old part of south Burnaby, a city just outside of Vancouver. We lived in an old rental apartment complex with many other immigrant families. At that time, there was a sense of community amongst us. We were all going through a similar phase in our lives. For most of these families, the parents were older and were at a stage in their lives that they only lived their hopes and dreams through their children. Several other Afghan immigrant families who lived near us remained part of our lives for decades to come.

At the age of seventeen, I wanted a car, just like any other high school student. My father, who had given us all that he could, continued his support by purchasing my first car, despite not having much money. A 1979 Ford Fairmont was not a popular car for a teenager even in 1991, however, I appreciated having a car to drive to school and work and looked at it as a privilege. I would start this car about ten minutes before we had to leave because the old engine would shut off if I put the car in gear too soon. I often packed it full of whoever needed a ride from the neighbourhood and would drive us all to school. Squeezing seven of us in that old car was the norm. Our ten-minute drive to school was always fun. I know that once we arrived at school some kids would laugh at us and call my car a boat as we pulled up to unload everyone. Despite being the subject of these jokes, we didn't care. I was just happy that I had a car and those who commuted with us had a blast listening to loud music during our short drive, just like any car full of teenagers.

As I continued to attend high school, I wasn't entirely sure how quickly I would learn English. I knew that no matter what, I would do my best to graduate high school. Studying to learn English starting in grade ten and completing the mandatory courses in high school to finish my first year of school in Canada was challenging. I struggled with subjects such as physics, social studies and others which required a certain level of English composition to be able to understand the class material. On the other hand, my elective courses such as photography, mechanics, and electronics were fun and easy. While other students were making the most of their lunch hour by socializing with friends, I dedicated this time to studying. The library became my lunch hour hangout. For my sister and I, eating our homemade sandwiches with our faces in a book became the norm.

Despite being envious of the other students who did not have to worry about struggling to learn a new language and adjust to life in a new country, I kept my focus on improving my English. As time went on and with the help of my amazing teachers, who truly cared and took the extra time to help me, I knew I was making substantial progress in school. My confidence grew, and I pictured myself passing the provincial exams and graduating high school easily. The support of my family and the encouragement of my teachers also provided the added confidence to set my sights on pursuing a post secondary education.

I remember that, as high school graduation was getting close, students seemed preoccupied with grad photos, parties, prom, and all the excitement that comes with the milestone of finishing high school. I, however, felt out of place. I had been so focused on improving my language abilities and maintaining a job after school that I never really had the opportunity to make many friends in high school. So, as graduation season came and went, I didn't really see much point in taking part in any of the grad related celebrations.

Graduation from high school was a great step toward my future as a Canadian. I had achieved enough of a grade point average to meet the basic requirements for entering a post secondary institution. I applied to several post secondary institutions, but, given my average grades and my limited English writing skills, I was not overly optimistic about being accepted into any post secondary institution. I became excited once I received acceptance letters from several institutions.

The pursuit of a higher education that might lead to a better future was only a dream for me at the beginning. I knew that I was just beginning to learn a new language and accept a new way of life in Canada. I was not sure how far I would progress in my education or what type of work I would be involved in to make a living. I knew that my parents had done everything they could to encourage us to work hard and get on a path which could lead us to a better life. The rest was up to us. I also knew that all I needed was the opportunity. By this time, I believed that making the best out of every moment in life had to become part of who I was. For over two decades after completing high school I do not remember ever having a week off during which I had nothing to do. I was always consumed by work, school, or both. This type of work ethic and mindset had its benefits and rewards. People like me can lose sight of balance in life because in everything we do, we give all that we have. This contributes to setbacks and losses in other areas of life and we eventually pay the price.

Just like most immigrants who want to normalize their life in Canada as quickly as possible with a goal of achieving stability in their new homeland, I was in a hurry to finish post secondary education and join the workforce. The slow pace of my initial two years in college studying business administration discouraged me a little. I had my sights set on becoming a Certified General Accountant. I partially chose this because I was good at understanding business and money management; I also chose this because my father had spent much of his life working in accounting. However, I had not fully researched the profession until my second year in business administration. I did not feel passionate about it. I also realized that those I wanted to meet and help were not likely to walk into a business office. I wanted to work with people who faced struggles in their lives.

## Finding a job with a sense of purpose

After changing my educational goals and stepping away from the business world, I set out to become a police officer. I mostly chose this job because I thought it would be challenging and rewarding at the same time. I knew that if I chose a job that required doing the same predictable thing everyday, I would get bored. I was also young at this time and thought that excitement was part of being a policeman and I would enjoy the adrenalin rush. At this stage, I never thought of how much negativity and trauma this job might expose me to. While preparing myself to qualify as an applicant, I continued to work and educate myself and volunteered as a Victim Assistance Worker. The five years of victim services experience was my first glimpse at the world of policing, and it gave me a chance to have an intimate look at the lives of those who were hurt by crime. I also researched the requirements for becoming a police officer. My first choice was the Vancouver Police Department. At that time, aside from the basic requirements, the Vancouver Police Department required applicants to pass a swimming test. Not being able to swim at the age of twenty-two temporarily stumped me. Things like learning how to swim was part of a kid's normal life in Kabul prior to the war. Those who were older than me, like some of my cousins and my uncles, all knew how to swim and some were expert swimmers because their childhood had been during times of peace. Yet when the war started, things like learning how to swim became an unnecessary luxury for most kids including me.

Learning how to swim as a twenty-two-year-old in a public pool was awkward and uncomfortable, but I adopted a new way of thinking and just stopped caring about what anyone else thought. Being shy and timid were no longer part of my life. Trying to not drown in a public pool as a grown man while trying to learn to swim with the help of a few swimming lessons was kind of hilarious. I often found myself laughing at my struggles with the basics of swimming in such a public place and couldn't help but look at children who swam around me trying to avoid me because sometimes I could get struck in the middle of a lane and frantically searched for the nearest edge of the pool to swim to before I found myself at the bottom of the pool. Despite all this, no lifeguard ever had to rescue me and eventually, I was a proud, self-taught swimmer, able to no longer sink in the water, but that's as far as I got.

## My first police uniform - the excitement

As I filled out an application package to become a police officer with the Vancouver Police Department (VPD) in 1998, I never imagined the journey this line of work would take me on. I had a basic understanding of police work, but what excited me most was that it would be an interesting job with lots of challenges. At the age of twenty-three, I never thought about some of the negative physical and psychological toll this job takes on young men and women who chose this line of work. Often, police officers find themselves in rough psychological shape at the end of their careers. This is something I later experienced as the years turned to almost two decades and self-care became a priority for me.

After having been in Canada for about eight years, I was proud of myself to pass all the requirements, interviews, and take part in the basic training program as a Reserve officer with the VPD. The Reserve program allowed me to gain some experience and better prepare myself to become a full-time police officer. In those days, the Reserve

Police officers of the VPD were fitted with old police uniforms that regular police officers were no longer wearing—in short, a second-hand police uniform. The fitting process also felt like browsing a second-hand clothing store, because we had to try on anything that was lying around in the equipment room and find pieces of the uniform that fit us. For a young and excited aspiring police officer, the second-hand uniform was just as cool as a brand new one. Our Reserve Academy class was held in the evenings and some weekends to accommodate for our regular lives in which most of us had other jobs or school. I, for one, was finishing post secondary courses at night in a part-time program toward finishing a diploma and working full-time as a restaurant manager.

Our classroom training consisted of basic legal and charter of rights training. We also spent some time learning the defensive tactics required for the job. Despite growing up in a challenging environment, I had never physically fought anyone. The violence I was subjected to did not take place in Afghanistan, which is deemed a violent and scary place to many people. All my confrontations and fights took place in Canada, and they were all while I was working as a police officer. Our classes were basic, focusing only on what we needed to know. I later learned that in jobs like policing, training is often limited to what you really need to know; the rest was up to the individual to learn. Normally, a commitment of personal time and effort was required if one wanted to expand their skills beyond the basics. After we arrived in Canada, I never thought that I would find myself holding a gun or taking part in any sort of a situation that involved violence of any type, yet here I was, willingly learning to use physical or deadly force.

Unlike my first introduction to a gun, which took about five minutes as we passed through the mountains of Afghanistan in 1989, this time I spent many hours and fired thousands of rounds of ammunition at the police firearms range. Our skilled instructors spent a lot of time explaining the safe handling and use of a firearm. At the time, the .39 specials or the revolver guns were no longer used by the regular Vancouver Police officers and handed down to us to use. I was impressed with the level of care and attention the instructors took to ensure that we did not take the responsibility of carrying a gun lightly. It was during my training with the VPD Reserves that I realized that, despite this being a part-time opportunity to take part in a limited area of policing, we still had the ability to affect the lives of those we came across. And given how life is valued much more in Canada than in Afghanistan, I appreciated this level of care and seriousness about a line of work where you cannot afford to be careless. I took all that came with being a Reserve Constable of the VPD very seriously.

Traffic direction was one of the main duties assigned to us as Reserve Officers of the VPD. I became comfortable wearing old motorcycle helmets and standing in the middle of a busy intersection such as Main Street and Terminal Avenue during a special event such as the Symphony of Fire. Waving by thousand of cars and people literally dancing around in the middle of an intersection gave me a unique look at what life was like for a VPD officer. But I enjoyed the long, exhausting shifts. The work seemed exciting and I was proud to be part of a police department in a major Canadian city. I felt that this was another big step for me as an immigrant in my journey to becoming fully integrated into society. For the next two years, I was able to take part, as part of my duties, in almost every major event such as hockey and football games and many concerts. Even though I knew that, as Reserve Officers, we were only considered peace officers and had limited exposure to police work, I still thought it was tons of fun. Other than breaking up an odd fight or making a routine arrest, my experience on the streets of Vancouver did not involve any significant incidents or events.

## Through an immigrant's lens

As my time progressed with the Vancouver Police Reserve, a unique opportunity presented itself where we were employed by the VPD as Police Custodial Guards. As a young man who wanted to learn all I could and immerse myself into the world of policing, I welcomed the opportunity and happily accepted a job as a part-time Police Custodial Guard. This experience opened my eyes as, for the next two years, I saw a sad and desperate side of life in Canada.

Downtown Eastside Vancouver has been described as one of the largest concentrations of drug addicts and homeless people in North America. It has been the subject of many studies and well-known documentaries. It scares some people, to the point where some refuse to even go there. Others lock their car doors as they pass through and many people think it is unsafe to even walk on the streets. This marginalized community of humans who call the Downtown Eastside home have often been judged by the larger community from what they have seen on their TV or, at best, out of their car windows as they drove by.

I have stories about members of this community, stories that came from walking amongst them, taking care of them, fighting with them, helping them, feeding them, and shaking their hands. I learned so much about the Downtown Eastside from working as a Police Custodial Guard (PCG) for the Vancouver Police Department in 1999, and ironically, I found myself there looking like them and smelling like them, trying to buy drugs on these streets over a decade later during an undercover training course. The decade that went by in this area did not change anything for these people though. The smells, sounds, and faces filled with despair were still the same and those who crowded the alleyways surrounding the corner of Main and Hastings Street all seemed familiar to me.

It was not until many years later that I realized how valuable was the experience I had gained by working in Vancouver's Downtown Eastside, more so than all my police training and all the courses I later took as part of this job. This experience helped me connect with people in crisis at a human level. This experience was about human suffering, how society looked at those who suffered, and how they responded to their needs. I was surprised to find this many Canadians in crisis. Seeing what I had seen so far in Canada did not prepare me to witness something like this. I felt that their daily struggle for survival, compared to my life as an immigrant, was much more difficult. Re-establishing our life as an immigrant family, which included living in a clean and safe apartment and having the ability to feed and clothe ourselves, seemed like a life of luxury compared to the despair faced by those who lived on the streets of Vancouver.

At this stage in my life, I realized that my stories of being an immigrant and coming from a war-torn country where people suffered and lived very difficult lives was not that much worse than those of people who live in Vancouver's Downtown Eastside. I began to think that I had something in common with the drug addicts and homeless of Downtown Eastside. I felt like I understood them, I did not judge them, and was often curious why they had ended up on the streets. A narrow-minded conclusion of summing up their lives as people who made a series of bad choices and ended up on the streets was not acceptable to me. However, I found that most of society, especially those in policing, often summed up a person's life in a few sentences because they only used their own sheltered lives and limited life experiences to arrive at such conclusions.

A few years after starting to work as a PCG, in my work with the RCMP, I often clashed with those who used their simplistic views about life to distinguish good guys from bad guys and good neighbourhoods from bad ones. I almost fell into the trap by adapting the lingo of referring to those accused of or suspected of committing crimes as "rats". This unacceptable term has been used for many generations in the police culture to describe those who find themselves at odd with the police. Unfortunately, I even used this demeaning term at times while speaking with my colleagues. As I matured, I realized how wrong this was. Summing up a human being's life without understanding the complexities they faced which ultimately brought them to a point of despair or criminality does not reduce them to be called rats. As society expects more from their police, fortunately some of these bad habits are starting to change in police work.

My job as a Police Custodial Guard was simple: take over custody of prisoners from the Vancouver Police officers, remove their handcuffs, search them, book them into the arrest and booking system and place them in their cell block. The only other part of the job was to feed the prisoners, occasionally facilitate their phone calls and fingerprint them. Learning these procedures and the other mechanical parts of the jobs was relatively easy, and for those who did it over many years, it was an almost robotic system where they didn't really concern themselves with the human element and just did their job. I, on the other hand, was all about the human element.

In this job, I interacted with some of the most difficult people I had ever met. They were also some of the most vulnerable, hurt, abused, desperate, drug addicted and mentally injured people. Here I learned how to be compassionate to those who made it difficult for anyone to work with them. At times, no matter how much you cared and tried to understand them, they were still difficult to deal with. Having suffered a life of misery, many of those who ended up in this jail were living on the streets and often arrested for petty crimes.

A key part of my new reality was adopting a strategy where I looked at this job as part of my education and preparation to becoming, one day, an effective police officer. For the most part, I did not let the negativity get the better of me. I thought that seeing the despair and difficulty and learning how to interact with those who are at their saddest and maddest when they entered the jail facility was more valuable than any course or training I would ever complete. This was also my first chance to see how those who were in the daily business of law enforcement managed to stay positive. Unfortunately, police culture breeds things like judging people quickly, a rigid belief in what is right or wrong, and looking down on non-conformists. Many of these attitudes also resulted in treating people poorly, with little compassion and understanding. I had to find my own way of staying positive by looking at this more as a helping profession than an enforcement job.

My experiences from war and the teachings of my parents were two key components of my continued compassion for humans. As my colleagues learned more about my background, I would hear things such as: "You must think this country and the problems these people come here with are a joke compared to Afghanistan." I found that people's perceptions were often skewed because of their assumption that those who come from tough places must also have rock-hard hearts. I would often respond to my colleagues by telling them that no matter what people see in their life or childhood, their heart still needs to have room for understanding towards others. Being a human first helped me connect with some of the most difficult and uncooperative prisoners during my two years of working at the VPD jail. My experiences as a kid who grew up during a war provided me with an increased capacity to take on lots and not complain much.

I can say for certain that for most of my life, my mental toughness got me through the challenges of working with humans in crisis. However, I only realized many years later that although the tough outer shell enabled me to be consumed and focused on what was happening with others, but it did not diminish the psychological trauma. Because I was able to take on much more than the average police officer, I often forgot about what was happening with me. It wasn't until almost twenty years later that I asked myself for the first time the question: What type of damage has police work caused me? What was happening to me every time I had to deal with gruesome and highly disturbing situations? I realized that I had a very soft heart. I cared about every victim, every family, and, yes, even the criminals whose mistakes often altered their life forever. Most of these people and situations stayed on my mind for years.

The men and women who worked with me at the VPD jail are the only ones who can describe the ongoing smells, sounds, and violence that took place there every day. Despite my background of being from what people refer to as a third world country, some of the things I experienced for the first time in Canada, a so-called first world country, were much worse than anything I had ever seen in my life.

A typical workday would start with me parking my car in the parking lot on Cordova Street, then I would walk among those who lived in the Downtown Eastside for a few minutes to make it to work at the old VPD station at 312 Main Street in Vancouver. This police station was one of the original fixtures of the City of Vancouver and was eventually condemned. After changing into my uniform and getting ready for my shift, which was completely different every time, I would enter our work area. The first thing about this place was the smell. Imagine entering an indoor facility where people have been coming and going for decades; the mixture of body odour, beer, hard liquor, marihuana, vomit, urine, and feces was the signature smell of the old VPD jail.

Those who had entered this facility even once would likely never forget this unique yet powerful odour. I felt that these odours permeated this jail without a chance to escape; it was like they were an entity attaching themselves to the very fixtures of the place. Even the walls smelled of it. The rule was not to touch anything with bare hands. Given that most of our prisoners came from a population who were living a high-risk lifestyle, many were infected with diseases that could easily be communicated to us while interacting with them. The jail was so old that each prisoner cells were divided by metal bars, making the expression behind bars a true statement. As time went on, the bars were almost nonexistent in most prisons and were replaced by walls, and the door was an actual metal door, but in 1999, if you went to jail in Vancouver, you experienced a real old-fashioned jail experience. The notion of deterrence never resonated with me while I worked in this jail. Despite the terrible conditions, the same people kept coming back day after day and week after week.

The first clue that we were about to receive another prisoner was the sound of the noisy and clunky elevator doors opening on the jail floor. As the VPD wagon drivers would escort the prisoners to the jail floor, we would greet them and take over. I would get ready for the type of prisoner I was about to deal with as soon as the door opened. There were three types of exits out of that elevator. There was the profanity shouting, fighting and kicking type whom we knew we clearly had to physically restrain, so a few of us would prepare to handle this type of a prisoner. Then there was the silent, almost unconscious type of prisoners; the police officers would often ask for help to drag them out of the elevator and into the famous drunk tank. Finally, there were those who walked in with a look of disbelief because they were there for something benign, like a warrant for too many outstanding parking tickets. We would often shame those officers who brought the seemingly normal citizens, such as the parking ticket delinquents, to this place. We thought there had to be a better way to deal with them rather than subjecting them to a visit with us.

A dark sense of humour carried us through most of the shift and we would try to joke even with the most violent prisoners by telling them that this jail was the best rated hotel they could get for the night given their actions, so why not make the best of it. We would tell our prisoners that a warm meat pie and a cup of coffee or a glass of juice was on the menu almost every lunch and dinner. I made these jokes with the prisoners with respect and they knew that I was trying to cheer them up during their trying times. The odd prisoner would not be impressed with this sense of humour, but you will always have those who don't see any humour about the dark side of life. But humour only carried me for so long until some experiences became just plain disturbing.

A few months into the job as a police custodial guard, I found myself trying to control a naked woman under the influence of drugs. How can this happen? As much as those who prepared schedules tried to always have a female custodial guard present during every single shift, there were very few women working with us. In 1998, the number of females interested in doing the type of work that had almost exclusively been a man's job for over a hundred years was still small, so there were situations where men had to interact with female prisoners under the most awkward of circumstances. Once such occasion was when a female who was arrested for something petty was brought to the jail and had to be searched for illegal drugs because she had a history of drug use.

During the shifts when no female jail guards were working, we always relied on the female nurse on duty to assist us with invasive searches involving female prisoners. The protocol was to place the female prisoner inside the cell block that was used for invasive searches, then the jail guard would stand by just outside of the door to ensure that the nurse was safe inside as she searched the prisoner. For the most part, this protocol worked without many incidents. This time things worked a little differently. After booking a female who lived on the streets of the downtown Eastside, it was my job to be the guard standing by the door as she was about to be searched by our nurse.

Me:        Ok, ready for this one? I must warn you that she is pretty worked up about this search, but I think I have reasoned with her and explained why we must search, so she should not give you any problems.

Nurse:     No problem. I'm sure this is no different than the other hundreds of these I have done over the years.

*Nurse steps into the cell.*

Nurse:     Hey there, I'm the nurse on duty here in the jail and I have to search you, ok? Has to be done, it's just part of the rules here. I'm sure you know that.

Prisoner:  Fine, fine. Let's just get this over with.

Nurse:     Bari over there will be standing by the door because he has to make sure we are safe, but he'll look away, so we have privacy, sounds good?

Prisoner:  Sure, whatever.

Nurse:     Open your mouth, lift your tongue, and let's check your ears, good. I have to check under your bra, too.

Prisoner:  Here, take a good look. See, I got nothing.

Nurse:     Ok great, almost done. Now I have to check your underpants.

Prisoner: Fuck you, bitch, get away from me!

*Sound of a chair being pushed.*

Me:        Is everything okay?

Nurse:     What are you hiding there?

Prisoner: Nothing, there is nothing there, now go away, bitch!

The nurse starts to step away as the prisoner throws a chair at her but misses. The commotion gets everyone's attention and I rush into the room to restrain her and she runs at me, pushing the chair into my shins. I lose my balance for a second, tripping face first on the floor. I land close enough to her bare and dirty feet to set her up perfectly to kick me in the face if she wanted to. But despite her violent behaviour, she chose not to kick me. I use the wall to push myself away from her feet and roll up quickly as I yell at her: "STOP!" I quickly restrain both her arms and hold her against the wall until others arrive. The nurse quickly leaves the room out of fear for her safety and my fellow guards run in. We get the prisoner under control. She starts to apologize immediately. As we all catch our breath, I ask her what type of drugs she has hidden inside her cavity. She tells me it's just down, and only two balls.

Down was the street name for heroin at that time. Heroin was often sold in tiny plastic wraps rolled into a ball in various quantities measured in grams. I say to her that if she does not take it out and hand it over to us, we have to keep her restrained and call a female police officer who has to come in and take it out for her. I tell her to smarten up and give me the drugs now.

Prisoner:    Ok, fine. Just let one of my hands go and I'll take it out.

*She reaches down between her legs, pulls three small balls of drugs out and hands them to me.*

Thanks to the rule of wearing latex gloves at all time, I am able to immediately take the drugs from her. We place her into her cell, and she puts her clothes back on. Things are calm again.

I tell my colleagues that I never had to do something this crazy before. They laugh and tell me it's just because I am new, and that this sort of thing happens here all the time. Addicts go through these extents to hide their drugs because if they lose them here, they have to go back out there and commit crimes to get the money they need and buy more. I tell my colleagues that we are really adding to the problem, then, by taking their drugs. "We aren't helping much, are we?" They laugh and ask me what choice we had, since it's against the law, plus if the prisoners decide to ingest it or the little plastic bags burst inside their body, they could die from an overdose.

As time went by, I got to experience more and more of what life was like inside a jail and how desperate some situations got for people who were caught up in the system. For the most part, I tried my best not to lay blame on the individuals and see their situation by looking at all the circumstances that led them to where they were. But in some situations, I could not help but to lay blame solely on the person. In these situations, my upbringing, morals and values could not let me see past the very important aspect of our behaviour as people and the choices we make every day.

One such time was when an extremely intoxicated man was so drunk and angry that, after being placed inside a temporary cell until he could be processed through the booking system, he had used the cell as a toilet and relieved himself fully on the floor of. During this extremely busy Friday night shift and after processing many prisoners, it was time to open the cell door and process this man. I was prepared for the smell from inside the cell and by this time, had developed enough tolerance to not gag or vomit. However, I was not prepared for a person trying to throw his feces at me because they were brought to jail for being extremely drunk. My quick reflex to push the small metal door back between the man and I saved me on that night from getting feces on me. This is not the type of thing anyone is ever prepared for. I was so mad at this guy that I did not care one bit about his state of drunkenness and the fact that his mind was altered. I only thought that no matter how drunk a person became, throwing feces at someone else could not be a choice any human would make. But I learned on this night that anything is truly possible.

At this point, I was still not fully familiar with all the laws and policies surrounding prisoners and was learning every day at a fast pace. After I shut the door, leaving the prisoner inside, I decided that the man was in urgent need of cleaning. I proceeded to find the water hose, which we normally used to clean vomit, urine, and any other bodily fluids from the floors and walls. This time, I was about to use the hose to wash down a prisoner. I began by running the water to its full strength then stood in front of the door holding the water into a nearby drain. I called upon one of my colleagues:

Me: Hey, can you come open this? I will try to make this quick.

Duty Sergeant: Emam, what the hell do you think you are doing?

Me: Trying to solve a problem, Sarg. What else can we do?

Duty Sergeant: Laughing: Are you nuts? Come over here.

*Colleagues laughing in the background.*

One colleague:     Rookie move, Emam, rookie move.

*I walk over to the main counter.*

Me:                I have to hose this guy down. He
                   tried to throw his shit at me, how
                   else can we deal with this guy?

Duty Sergeant:     Well, Emam, it's nice of you to force
                   a shower on this guy, but you can't.
                   He can complain that you forcefully
                   hosed him down and you will find
                   yourself being investigated for
                   trying to help this guy.

Me:                So, what do we do in a situation like
                   this?

Duty Sergeant:     Well, a few of us glove up, mask up,
                   and walk in. Ideally, restrain the
                   guy without fighting and talk him
                   into cleaning himself up. You can't
                   force anyone to do anything.

The Sergeant's explanation made sense. He had
been on the job for over twenty-five years and by all
accounts, had seen it all. So, his approach of trying to
reason with a person who was willing to throw feces
back at another person thought me that connecting

with people at their worst still comes down to looking at them as humans first.

Despite seeing many disturbing human behaviours over the next two years of being a police custodial guard for the VPD, it did not deter me from becoming a police officer. The way I looked at it was that someone had to deal with people at their worst and see the side of humans most of us would never see in our day to day lives. I also gained a huge amount of insight into some of the inner workings of a big city police department. I felt that this type of experience was important for anyone who was about to enter policing. Later in my job, I found that those who had dealt with some human tragedy were much better police officers versus those who lived sheltered lives. I also found that those who come from small towns and were exposed to a limited number of issues which were often not all that serious or life-changing quickly became overwhelmed with complicated issues. There is a certain toughness that big city cops have because of the array of issues they deal with on the streets; this was the reason that big city police work was appealing to me as a job that I could do for a long time and not be bored with.

In the end, the two years of being a Reserve officer and a custodial guard was all I did with the VPD, so I never got to experience what it was like to walk the beat in Downtown Eastside, but I did walk amongst and dealt with its residents and became very familiar with their lives and struggle.

Either at the end of a shift or going into work, I often found myself walking amongst the same people who had been fighting with us inside the jail and were now walking back outside. These people were always much nicer on the outside. Despite the difficult life they led, they were in their element on the streets, and most times they were slightly less pissed off and less intoxicated or under the influence of drugs. So, I liked seeing them out of jail. Some would recognize me and I would greet them as if we were acquaintances. Some would joke with me on their way out of jail by saying "Hope not to see you again today". This usually meant that I would eventually see them in a few days or in week's time. I found it sad that once I walked out of my job, I would walk to the parking lot of the Cordova Street to drive home to my apartment, yet those who were let out of jail would walk out and they were home. Calling a street corner home is a hard life; unfortunately, many people call those streets home to this day.

After about two years of working as a part time employee of the VPD and managing a small business as my fulltime job, I knew that I had gained much of the valuable experience necessary to start looking for a full-time job as a police officer. Ideally, I wanted to stay in the Lower Mainland, but given the slow pace of hiring at that time with municipal departments, I did not have the patience to wait. So, I applied to the RCMP.

After meeting their minimum requirements, passing a relatively simple written test, physical abilities test, and an interview, I was called by the recruiting people and asked if I was willing to go to Regina to attend the basic training, which would take about five months. Initially, I did not want to accept this. It was 2001, and although it had been over ten years since we had fled Afghanistan, I had no desire to leave my family again just to get a job after the ordeal we had been through. I reflected on this briefly and realized that even though I had little motivation to travel to Regina and go though the unpaid five-month training, I should probably go with it anyway as a last step to get myself a job I can be happy with. The notion that I could be posted anywhere in Canada did not set well with me either because the RCMP had this antiquated policy at that time and sent people away from their home provinces. And often, they had no good reason for it. Despite all this, I took my chances and hoped that I would come back to the Lower Mainland after completing the training.

In March 2001, I was packing my bags and getting ready to head back to the cold climate of Regina. Our initial arrival to Canada in Winnipeg had prepared me for this type of weather, so the windy and cold climate of Regina during the five months of training was not too bad. A taxi ride from the airport to the training academy, known as the Depot or what we jokingly referred to as the Farm, put me in a strange environment. Learning the basics of what I needed to know to perform the job of a police officer was a breeze, but the paramilitary culture of the institution and the teaching methods completely threw me off. I did not see it as the proper training for a job where you always interact with the Canadian public during your duties. I came to the Depot with what they called bad habits. I had developed those habits in life and my two years of experiencing the police culture with the VPD. I quickly realized that that RCMP was not very open to accepting the way anyone else did business; they were set in their ways and that became evident to me as I made my way through the training program. However, I was there and had made a commitment to finish this training and get a job, so I stayed the course.

## My first day of training in police academy

It was during our first official day of class that I saw what they call a rigid drill Sergeant at work. Up to this point, I had only seen movies about this sort of a thing, mostly funny movies where a guy is yelling at the top of his lungs at a group of wide-eyed young men and women at some military facility to toughen them up. I didn't think this type of thing happened, especially in a police training facility. Before applying for this job, I had educated myself on the function of police within Canadian society, so I expected that we would learn how to respectfully and effectively interact with people, solve problems, and build relationships with communities, among many other things.

Given the life I had been through this far, I was never one to sit stiff as a board, so I must have been looking too relaxed once the drill instructor walked into the class to give us the dress and deportment lecture. As a grown man sitting in a class full of other grown men and women, I was surprised that this instructor was talking to us like we were little kids. For the first bit of his lecture, I thought this was a joke and the guy would snap out of it and say something else, like: "This is an adult learning environment and if we are going to trust all of you to carry guns, make life and death decisions, and be responsible for affecting people's lives in a significant way once you become police officers, then we trust that you know how to make your beds, iron your clothes and be respectful of others." However, the drill instructor was not joking, so I began to worry a little about what the rest of the training might be like.

At one point during the drill instructor's lecture, I smirked at one of his comments and looked around to see if anyone else felt the same way. He must have seen the look on my face. Minutes after, he walked up to me saying: "Elvis is dead, yes, he is dead. Did you get that? Elvis is dead." I was about to say: "What is your problem and why are you telling me about Elvis?" My look of confusion got the attention of one of the instructors who was not a drill guy; he was a much kinder and more experienced and taught us legal studies and other theory-based materials. He caught my eye, then pointed to his sideburns. I quickly realized that the loud drill instructor was telling me that my sideburns were too long, and I probably should get a haircut to look the way they wanted everyone to look. I nodded my head in an effort not to upset the drill instructor anymore and he walked away.

He continued to go on about how, from this day on, we would do what we were told and when we were told and not question anything, because many others have gone through this before to earn the right to carry the badge and so on. This was my first introduction to what later we all called playing the game, of pretending to obey every silly little thing the drill instructors told us and not being offended while we were treated like children, so that we didn't piss them off. If we did upset the drill people, they had the ability to make our lives at the training academy difficult. I found this disappointing; after all, I thought we were about to embark on a journey on which we were going to be trusted with people's lives and using our own judgement, creativity, and unique skills which we brought to the class should have been valued. I was never sold on the philosophy which I think was basically telling aspiring police officers to leave their brains behind and just blindly follow what they were told, because they will be taught everything they needed to know.

One of the most valuable parts of this training was living with and getting to know my fellow Cadets who had travelled to Regina from all corners of Canada. I found that every one of us had a unique background and came from a different walk of life, but we were all Canadians. This was my first opportunity to notice the differences in culture between everyone. I learned that Canadians share many common values, but that there were some stark differences between people depending on which part of this vast country they came from. For example, a young man from Montreal was completely different than the person from a small northern town in the Prairies.

I appreciated the diversity of our class and realized that even those who come from other countries are not that different from those born and raised in various parts of Canada. I found myself easily adapting to the small city of Regina compared to the person who had spend their entire life in a big Canadian city like Toronto, Montreal or Vancouver, because I had lived in Winnipeg for about a year. This was the first time I saw the power of integration versus assimilation. Everyone in the class brought something unique and valuable with them from their respective backgrounds. Despite the philosophy of the training academy to make us all the same at the end, most of us never really changed who we were as people, but our behaviour did change to reflect the needs and expectations of the job.

I learned a lot about people from those who went through the training academy. We saw that, when combined, our unique strengths were much more valuable, and we managed to help each other during challenging times. This is something we realized as a class, not something which was ever really emphasized as part of the training. Our natural ability as people who came together from all corners of Canada helped us connect with each other and see the value in our diversity. After meeting these wonderful people, I was hopeful for the future of immigrants in Canada, because I felt that no matter which corner of the country they came from, Canadians were for the most part respectful of those who were different.

Unfortunately, the police academy did not provide any training about diversity, cultural sensitivity, or the importance of understanding Canada's demographics. In my opinion, this lack of training translated at times into the deployment of ineffective police officers to communities which they knew nothing about. The burden was often put on the individual to learn about the communities they policed. In my view, this has been part of the problem in policing when it comes to gaining the trust and respect of communities who are different than the norm. In my opinion, the philosophy that a new Mountie who just finish the training in Regina can fit into any community or anywhere in Canada was flawed.

I was about halfway finished with the training where I became nervous about my first posting. What if I was posted somewhere other than the Lower Mainland of BC? I never wanted to quit, but I thought that if I did not get back to work in the same province as my family, then I would likely quit. To me, no job was so important for me to abandon my family or home. Not long after the halfway mark, I learned that I would be going back to BC, so I was happy and continued to focus on finishing the training. Unfortunately, some of my classmates were posted in locations where the look in their faces spoke volumes about how disappointed they were to go there after the completion of the training. This was especially hard for those who were established in a community, had children attending school, and had their family roots for many generations in one area.

The five months of training went by quickly and we were all excited to get out of the academy and get back to the real world and, most importantly, back to our lives and families. Despite some of the issues with the training style of the RCMP, the instructors did a great job of teaching us the mechanical skills of becoming proficient with the use of firearms, physical control of persons, basics of investigations, emergency vehicle operation, and other basic necessary skills every police officer must have to safely perform their front-line duties.

The long hours of polishing leather boots and the accessories that were part of our dress uniform took valuable time away from our training, but I guess it also served some purpose every time I wore the uniform for a ceremony that represented the organization well. My perspective was slightly off from the wide-eyed young men and women who were so proud to show off their shiny boots and red uniform. I guess growing up with Mounties as part of Canada's history was the reason for their excitement and pride. As for me, my upbringing didn't include this history, so the red serge or any other police uniform were all the same to me. I felt that no matter what the uniform looked like, the most important part of this job was to provide a meaningful service to the public.

Packing up to go home and starting the job was an exciting moment in my life. Sleep deprivation was the number one complaint from almost everyone who attended the training academy. Aside from starting a new job, I was looking forward to sleeping in my own bed and, when I woke up, to chose not to make my bed if I so wish, and no one would care. I knew that there was so much about my character that would never change, but a few things did change about me once I completed this training. My family and friends noticed these changes immediately. I became more reserved, cautious about my association with others, selective about attending any social events and highly focused on the job. I guess I took the job too seriously, just like most new police officers do. As I became more seasoned and gained more life experience, I realized that production line police training and attempting to make robots out of humans was the worst thing about being a cop. Trying to undo this damage takes a lot of personal reflection and work, which is often done after police officers have left the job and realizing that they feel out of place in many of life's circumstances. This is especially true for those police officers who were employed by organizations almost entirely focused on maintaining their image and neglecting the human element, leaving us, in the end, with great mechanical but a suffering human side.

All of these were good things for a new police officer and a benefit to the police agency. Unfortunately, later in life, most police officers suffer negative consequences in their personal lives because of this job. Getting sucked into the life of being a cop most of the time was one of the prices I paid by choosing police work. This happens to many young men and women, where the job becomes nearly all-consuming. We often operate in a state of hyper vigilance. Police culture does not necessarily promote a healthy balance of ensuring that the job does not negatively affect the personal lives of police officers. Like many other companies, they praised arduous work, long hours, dedication, and making personal sacrifices to benefit the organization.

## Life as a new police officer

In September 2001, I was the only Afghan-born Canadian serving as a police officer in BC. The number of police officers from the Middle East were very few in all of Canada at that time. More men and women of Middle Eastern descent have joined various police agencies across Canada since. However, the numbers are still very small. I knew that police work was not one of those jobs that ever had much appeal to people from the Middle East, so I never expected to come across many police officers from my ethnic background. At the time of writing, it has been almost twenty years since I started working in this capacity, and not much has changed in this regard.

By 2001, Afghanistan was one of those countries that people had forgotten about. Because the stories surrounding Afghanistan were mostly from the 1980s and the early 90s, I never expected people to know much about Afghanistan. About a week into my new job as a police officer, the images of planes crashing into buildings in New York brought Afghanistan back into the spotlight very quickly. It wasn't long before people's curiosity about Afghanistan started to affect me. Suddenly, I became a much more interesting person to those I worked with. I realized that every time a small country like Afghanistan is introduced, especially in a negative way, people's imagination runs wild and their perceptions form quickly just by watching the news. I realized that not many people knew any facts about Afghanistan. I found myself educating others and trying to explain to them that a little country such as Afghanistan should not be the sole focus of terrorism talk, but the complexities surrounding this issue and the ugly political games played for decades did not seem to matter to many people. They were trying to make sense of and talk about solutions in relation to a part of the world whose history goes back a few thousand years and whose present is wrapped in complexities which can only be discussed intelligently with a historian who can understand that part of the world.

As emotions ran high in North America about terrorism after the attacks on the United States, I saw the shift in people's attitudes towards those from the Middle East. As a front-line police officer, I wasn't sure what to expect. I tried to understand everyone's vigilance about terrorism but, at the same time, was surprised by the ignorance of some. One day, I was sent to a call where a person had called the police because two suspicious Middle Eastern people were sitting in a car and looking at flight manuals. I thought to myself that it couldn't be for real, after the world watched the events of September 11th, it is unlikely that two Middle Eastern persons would use the same method days after to come up with a terrorist plot while sitting in their car in North Vancouver, of all places.

I thought that maybe because I was born in Afghanistan and was new on the job, the dispatchers were playing a joke on me. The workplace was a lot less sensitive to ethnic matters in those days, so the types of jokes cops played on each other could easily include something like this. As I started to laugh it off, I realized that this was not a joke, it was an actual call to the police that I had to investigate. So, I drove up to the area and searched for the car. I found it parked in a lot near a travel agency. Inside were a young Persian couple who were looking at vacation brochures which they had just picked up from the travel agency. At this point, I had to pause and reflect. My training was such that I had to speak with them to rule them out as "suspicious" people, which meant that I had to obtain their names, addresses, and contact information, then enter them into the police computer. This means that their names and this incident would stay in the police database for years. I realized that this way of doing business was simply stupid. Why would I do this, if my common sense and facts dictated otherwise? Besides, I realized that, under the Charter of Rights, I would be arbitrarily detaining these people. I did not have a legal reason to even speak to the couple. So, I ignored policy and training and did what was right. I left them alone and drove away.

For the next fifteen years or so, Afghanistan became a very familiar name to many Canadians and to the rest of the world, especially after Western countries invaded it. The war on terror started, with an overwhelming number of negative images and stories from Afghanistan. Aside from the curiosity of people and answering questions I received, I knew that there was not much I could do to explain the complexities of why Afghanistan was in such a mess for decades.

For many years, I shared my perspective with people about life, the difficulties other parts of the world faced, and living in peace versus war. Early on in my job, there were many occasions where I felt that people's problems in Canada were so minor. I thought to myself that people have been spoiled because they have everything in Canada. I asked myself about why Canadians would find petty things to complain about and make them into large issues. As I matured and understood more about human nature, I became more understanding and realised that I had to meet people where they are. So, I never belittled or trivialized any sort of a problem on the job. This included 9-1-1 call which sometimes were related to objectively minor issues, but were important and urgent enough for some individuals to send them into a state of panic, so they called for help—such as the Persian couple leafing through travel pamphlets. I had to attend many such calls for service during my first three years of being a uniformed police officer to problem solve and assist those who needed it. A good example of the minor issues that became a big deal was a neighbour dispute, and I was disappointed with the lack of skill and ability of two neighbours who could not solve a minor issue between themselves.

As a young officer, I never understood why the police would have to show up and have these conversations with people. Many times, I thought about asking people if they forgot or lost the skill to talk to other human beings about small problems. But I never did. Time and time again, I reminded myself of the promise I had made that no matter what, I should never compare or belittle the difficulties and experiences of those whom I came across with as a Canadian police officer.

In my three years of uniformed police work, I had the opportunity to problem solve regularly and come across many situations where there was no training for. I learned how to reason with people and gain cooperation. Some decided to fight, some pulled out a weapon and some were simply helpless and did not know what to do. I did my best to be compassionate toward the range of human behaviour and emotions I faced. Unfortunately, the culture and coping mechanism in police work sometimes takes away the compassion. On a personal level, I wanted to always be compassionate to others no matter who they were and what they had done. From a police culture perspective, being tough, sarcastic, judgemental, shrugging my shoulders, and laughing everything off was the more appropriate survival method, which I got sucked into. This internal clash of values made it very difficult for me to be a police officer for all the years I spent on the job. I knew that the job I was doing was important and someone had to do it, and the aspects of helping people made the job rewarding for me. However, I did not like who I was becoming.

There were many situations in which the safety and well being of others were under threat by the criminal actions of another. There were too many such incidents to name, so I will only share a few here. The most important moments where I felt that just being a compassionate human being was the only way to help someone were the rewarding moments that stayed with me.

These were two situations where a life was about to be lost and I happened to be the person wearing a uniform at that moment. I felt honoured to have been able to help someone whom I thought was very close to dying. In police culture, poking fun at firefighters by calling them bucket heads and at times at paramedics who might have disturbed a crime scene was a reality. Being part of several life-saving efforts made me realize that those who are not in the business of investigating but just want to rush in and save lives deserve the utmost respect. They truly care about people and are often traumatized by what they see.

## Stories of human struggle - from my eyes

## How quickly a life could be lost

It was a relatively quiet summer evening, and I was driving my police car. During slower nights, we didn't have to rush from one call to another, so I did what old fashion police work was all about. I drove around most of the night looking to find crime or at least try to be visible in areas where sometimes crimes occurred to prevent it from happening. On nights like these, the emergency calls normally alarmed me much quicker because often there was radio silence for extended periods of time, so the loudly urgent calls often shocked my system. My reaction to such calls always started by an elevation in my heart rate, which increased my state of alertness, followed by a desire to rush to the area where the emergency call was coming from. The normal protocol was that the police dispatchers would call upon a specific police officer, referring to them by their unit number to respond to the call.

My unit number was often Bravo 9. For some reason, I never really waited for the dispatchers to assign me the call; as soon as such emergency calls came in, no matter where I was, I would start to drive toward the area where someone had called for help. The dispatchers would then often send me a message over the mobile workstation inside my police car, jokingly saying: "Of course you are en route". I found that most young and keen police officers carried themselves the same way by trying to race to answer calls as quickly as they could even though they were not called upon. This was a sense of duty and camaraderie, where we always wanted to help each other knowing that one of us was about to go into a situation where they might need help. This was one of the best parts of the job to me. No other job that I did in policing ever had the same level of self-sacrifice and camaraderie, and the best part of this was that almost everyone was junior officers and full of energy.

That night, the call came over the radio, piercing the peaceful silence loudly enough to get my heart rate going and I rushed to grab my mic to respond.

Dispatcher:     Stand by for a call of a suicidal female.

*A few moments of silence.*

Dispatcher:   All clear units start heading down toward the bridge.

Me:   Bravo 9 is close by and on the way.

Dispatcher:   Bravo 9 copy. Members attending be advised that the distraught female is on the bridge deck.

Me:   Bravo 9 is almost there; the park is closed. Are you sure she is on the bridge?

Dispatcher:   10-4, somehow, she has made it past the gates and is now in the middle of the bridge.

Me:   Copy, I'm in the parking lot and about to walk up to the front now.

Dispatcher:   Copy, give me an update ASAP, I am calling EHS (Emergency Health Services) to head to the parking lot.

As I walked past the gates, the person who had called in the emergency points me to where a young lady was, standing in the middle of the bridge. I can hear her saying something, but it is hard to hear. As I walked closer and vault over a fence, my heart rate starts to race. I started to see her face from a distance, but she seems familiar. She looks back and yells:

"Don't get any closer or I will jump, I swear I am not kidding!"

| Me: | Okay okay okay, I will stand right here. Please don't do anything. |
|---|---|

| Female: | Bari? Is that you? |
|---|---|

| Me, shocked to hear my name: | Yes. It's me. Are you ok? |
|---|---|

The first good sign in a situation like this is that the person is talking to me. For a moment, I froze. I could not recall who this young lady was or how she knew my name. Regardless, because I was walking towards her in a well-lit area and my shaved head and darker skin were usually the first giveaways, most people who knew me easily recognized me. I even wondered if this is a friend or a family member whom I failed to recognize. I get back on my police radio to communicate the situation.

| Me: | Dispatch, ready for an update. |
|---|---|

| Dispatch: | Go ahead Bravo 9. |
|---|---|

| Me: | I have the young lady on my sights and am starting to talk to her. |
|---|---|

I hear multiple sirens from a distance and see that the young lady is looking around in a panic. The sirens are distracting her, and I feel like I am losing her attention.

Me:              Dispatch, ask all the responding cars to turn off their lights and sirens. I want everyone to quietly arrive and wait in the parking lot. We don't need anyone else here right now. She's panicking.

Dispatch:    Copy Bravo 9.

I try to resume my conversation with the young lady.

Me, pretending that I        When did I see you last?
remember her:

Female:       I know you tried to help me last month when I was feeling depressed, but tonight things just got bad for me.

As soon as she said this, it all came back to me very quickly. I realized that about a month ago, I spoke with this young lady who was feeling suicidal, but we managed to talk about it and she seemed better and willing to get help, so at the end of our interaction, things worked out. I know that I now must remind her about our bond from last time and quickly gain her trust, so I can get on the bridge. But there isn't much time.

Me:      I remember that we had a great plan for what you would do if things got bad again. Can we talk about that? Would you be open to that? I am here to help.

Female:  I don't know Bari. This time, I really don't know. My hands are starting to get tired, and I'm scared.

As I shine my flashlight towards her, I realize that this situation is a lot worse than it seems. She has climbed over the railing onto the outside of the bridge and is barely hanging from the outside. She is holding the cable on the outer edges with both hands and she keeps looking down.

Me:      Can you please let me get closer to you, so that I can hear you better?

Female:  I don't know, Bari. I don't think I want anyone on this bridge right now.

Me:      If you let me get a little closer, I can hear you better. I can always walk backwards if you want me to go away. So, can I walk a little bit towards you just to hear your voice better?

Female:  Ok Bari, but don't get too close.

I walk about ten steps towards her as slowly as I can while trying not to shake the bridge. I take the biggest steps I can so that I can get as close to her as I can.

Female:        Stop. That's close enough, you can hear me from there Bari, don't get any closer.

Me:            Ok, I will stop.

I look her in the eyes; she looks terrified.

Me, smiling:   Hi.

Female, voice   Hi Bari. I think this time I really
shaking:       can't handle it. I really can't.

By this time, about five minutes have gone by and I know that she is scared and tired. My biggest concern is that if her arms cannot hold onto the railing any longer, she will plunge into the river under the bridge and I do not want to watch this. How could I live with myself knowing that I got within about twenty feet of a young lady and could not help her? So, I started to negotiate with her about why it was so important that she allow me to come even closer to her.

Me:     I know you are scared and I'm sure whatever is going on in your mind is overwhelming you. But I know from our talk last time that you have a lot to live for.

Female:   Like what?

Me:       Well, can we discuss that? Because I remember many things that you need to be around for. Like that perfect wedding you wanted to have one day, remember? And much more. (A few seconds of silence.) I will make a deal with you. If you let me come to you, you can hold onto me and I will stay with you as long as you want to. I really don't like standing where I am.

Female:   Are you trying to trick me, Bari? If I let you come close to me, then all the others will rush in and then what? I get arrested?

Me:       No, no, no. I am not tricking you. I know your arms are getting tired. So, can I just walk over there and help you stabilize a little. I will just listen and that's it, ok? I want to help. I am here for you. Do you trust me?

Female:   Yes, I trust you Bari.

After hearing her say this, I took one long breath of air into my lungs and then out which relieved some of the tension in my chest.

I take as many big steps as I can to get close to her. I find myself face to face with her. Without thinking, the first thing I do was to wrap my arms around her waist and hold onto her as tight as I can. I say to myself, "Now I've got her, and hopefully I have the arm and shoulder strength to hold onto her for a while." She's breathing heavily and I can feel the strong beat of her heart against my chest and her heavy breaths against my neck.

For the next twenty minutes, I talk to this young lady about life, and her struggles with mental health, the reasons she got onto the bridge that night and, most importantly, about hope. I did everything I could to convince her that she was a young and beautiful person, full of life, and that she had just had a moment which maybe took her to a place where she did not know what else to do. I related to her as a person and told her that every human being can find themselves exactly where she was if life circumstances bothered them to a point where they simply became overwhelmed.

As my arms and shoulders began to get tired, I started to feel nervous about my ability to hold onto her for much longer. I finally convinced her that my arms were getting weak, too, and that there was no way I was walking away from her, but that I needed help. I had to ask my colleagues for help and she agreed to let them onto the bridge. As I managed to keep her engaged in conversation, several of my colleagues rushed to get close to us.

She got startled and started to pull back from the railing. I realized that her incredible strength was enough to pull me up from my feet. Up to this point, I was standing solidly on my feet. The feeling that I was about to go over the railing and that she might drag us both down over 200 feet into the river sunk my heart for a moment. I felt the arm of a colleague on my shoulder and then realized that everyone was behind me.

I take a breath, and I tell everyone that we had to pull her up immediately.

I continued to look her in the eyes and saw a terrified young lady. She did not want to die that night. As we pulled her up over the railing and back inside the bridge railing, everyone was quick to try and restrain her. But I shoved them away and first gave her a hug.

"You are going to be ok," I told her.

The ambulance and other police officers walked her away from the bridge and she got the help needed that night from medical professionals and her family. I never saw her again, but I felt that her and this experience would stay with me for a long time.

As I walked back to my police car, I had the tough guy face of a police officer who now had to write the report and conclude the file then get ready for the next call. This time, once I sat inside my car by myself and all the noise went away, I felt a sense of relief followed by a feeling of extreme sadness. But my job was to leave this call behind and get ready for the next one, so I sucked it up and moved on. This became part of an unhealthy pattern for many years; the culture of policing expected us to walk around like robots, so it became part of my life as it does for most police officers. I later learned that there was nothing worse than suppressed emotions. This was such a contrast to the early part of my life when, as a young man, I was full of emotions about what I witnessed in Afghanistan and my family's journey away from our homeland. At that time, I felt all the pain, shed many tears, was sad, and became angry about the things I experienced. It took me almost two decades as a police officer to realize that I did not want to lose the emotional part of me because of this job. I could have managed all the trauma I experienced on the job much better if I had allowed the emotions to be experienced as they came.

## Please don't die on me, lady

Family disputes were one of the most common calls we answered as uniformed police officers. Most of these calls were related to minor disputes, where a mix of emotions and frustrations over everyday life issues just became too much and resulted in heated arguments. Loud arguments can become disturbing enough for neighbours to call the police—most often to make sure no one was getting hurt. Even though I was doing my best not to judge family dynamics in Canada, I thought that my values were so different than the society I was now a part of. For me, there were big differences between family values and conflict management in Canada compared to those from where I had come from.

I had attended many family disputes which had been helped by the presence of a police officer. At the end of these disputes, I felt that our presence helped a family deescalate a situation and find a resolution. I had never been to a family dispute call where our presence made things so much worse that a member of the family almost lost their life.

In frontline uniform police work, attending to emergency calls came first despite anything else we had going on. My night shifts started at 6 p.m. and continued until 6 a.m. After attending to several calls, completing the necessary paperwork and anything else that had to be completed, I often kept awake during the late hours of the night by making sure that I was not sitting in the office buried in paperwork and instead, stayed on the road as much as possible, and I was often the first one to rush to emergency calls. Driving fast with the flashing lights and the siren blaring was one way to keep me awake at night.

It was a cold, wet, rainy winter night, and the downpour of rain made emergency driving difficult. Driving too fast in the Ford Crown Victoria police car in these rainy nights made the cars hydroplane. On this night, the call came over the police radio as I was about to take a turn to pull into a restaurant for a dinner break in my usual police car, Bravo 9. Normally, if we just sat down for dinner, the dispatchers were very considerate and would try their best and not interrupt us during. They also knew our GPS locations and, because they worked with us for many years, they even knew our dinner habits. And yet, I got called by the dispatcher.

Dispatcher:     Bravo 9, I know you are about to pull
                in for dinner, but I need you.

Bravo 9:        No problem, go ahead with the call.

Dispatcher:     Neighbours hears a heated family
                argument and are concerned.

Bravo 9:        Copy, where am I going to?

*Dispatcher gives the location.*

Bravo 9:        Any history of this type of stuff at the
                address?

Dispatcher:     Negative, that is why the neighbours
                are concerned. This family has never
                had this type of a situation.

Bravo 9:        Copy.

Dispatcher:     Bravo 9, can you respond Code 3, I'm
                being told that things are escalating.

Bravo 9:        Copy, responding Code 3. Send me
                some cover please.

Every time I had to race to an emergency call
with lights and sirens, a few things happened
automatically. My heart rate started to increase, I
sat up straight on my seat, I often got warm as the
blood started to pump through my body, I turned

the music off to be able to listen fully to every detail that was communicated over the police radio, I checked to ensure that my seatbelt was on in case I crashed the police car, and, based on the information communicated to me over the police radio, I thought about what I could do as soon as I arrived. Most of the time, the information and all the thoughts in my head made me alert but never really helped until I faced the people who were in crisis.

Dispatcher:  Copy Bravo 9, I am sending you a cover car.

Bravo 9:  I'm a few minutes away.

I arrive at the address with my cover car behind me, pulling in almost at the same time. We walk up to the residence where the family dispute is taking place and can hear the loud voices of everyone inside. No one is threatening or saying anything of concern to us. I just hear a very upset family who is obviously having a tough time while trying to sort out some type of an argument.

As we enter the front door of the residence, all the yelling stops for a few seconds, every member of the family looks at us standing at their front door. The look in the faces of this family was one of disbelief. They all seemed shocked to see police at their door. Then they went back to yelling at each other. My fellow officer and I introduced ourselves amidst all the yelling and tried to explain to the family the reason for being there. Our effort to get their attention was not very effective and the yelling continued.

Our mere presence often helped people calm down in these situations, but not this time. They felt embarrassed and were concerned about their reputation. They could not accept that their actions caused someone to alert the police. As they continued to argue and as they asked us to leave their home, I noticed that the mother was changing colour, looking pale and lifeless. I see her jaw drop and she is reaching for something to hold onto, but she collapses onto the floor. All members of the family immediately begin to run to her, pulling and tugging to try and wake her up, all of them in a state of panic. I realize that this woman had just suffered a cardiac arrest. I rush to her side and pull several hands away from her upper body to check her vital signs. The only thing I hear is one of the family members yelling, "Oh my God, mom is dead", followed by a scream.

Auditory exclusion is a term used to describe how a person becomes so focused in dealing with what is in front of them that they don't hear anything else. This is exactly what happened to me. Other than hearing "Oh my God, mom is dead", I did not remember hearing anything else as I focused on the lifeless human body lying in front of me. I later learned that pulling family members from a person whose heart had just stopped and was no longer breathing became a challenge for my partner who somehow did this all on his own while I was attending to the collapsed woman. My partner later told me that he felt like the family's concern for their loved one had given them incredible strength to cling on to the body and his shoulders were sore after forcing everyone off the woman, so that I could administer CPR. Surprisingly, I did not see or remember any of this either. I used all the strength and focus I had to move the body in front of me to a position where I could be face to face with her and try to bring her back to life.

I was trained for this type of a situation. However, hearing the ribs of the woman break and seeing blood coming out of her mouth as I continued applied chest compressions and performed mouth to mouth resuscitation was an experience that I was not prepared for. The pale and lifeless body lay there in a helpless state as I continued to perform CPR for several minutes and looked to higher powers for help. I remember that I was beginning to sweat and that my heart rate was increasing as I tried to keep the chest compressions going. Because I was doing both chest compressions and mouth to mouth resuscitation, I tired quickly. Trying to keep this woman's heart pumping long enough and hoping that maybe she would come back was all I could think about.

After the ambulance arrived, I told my partner that I had blood on my face and clothes and that I needed to leave immediately. By this time, other police officers had arrived at our location. I walked to my police car and wiped my face and hands. As I drove to the hospital to check on the status of this person, I started to think about my return to her family. What would I say to them? How could I deliver the news that their mother was now dead because of a seemingly minor family argument?

Unfortunately, the negative lens that most police officers view the world through often interferes with their ability to see things in a hopeful and optimistic way. Not once did it occur to me that the woman might have survived. I arrived at the hospital. I go to the emergency room and try to find the attending doctor for a confirmation of death. A nurse I knew well, since I visited the emergency room many times as part of my duties, said: "Hey Bari, if you are here for the lady who just came in with a cardiac, she's in surgery." I look back and ask her: "What? Are you saying she's alive?" The nurse says: "Yes, Bari, we don't do surgery on dead people, you know." I smile at her and say thanks.

Statistics say that the chances of survival after a full cardiac arrest where the heart stops and the person is no longer breathing is about 10%, but these odds increase if CPR is administered right away. The woman was lucky to have collapsed in front of us. The ambulance crew told me that the CPR kept her heart pumping just long enough to keep her alive. Shortly after, they detected a heart rate and the doctors at the hospital operated on her immediately. A life was not lost that day because we happened to be there made me realized that I looked at the world too negatively at times. I also realized that, occasionally, I needed to clean my foggy and dark lens as a police officer and see things in a hopeful light. I thought about how much more optimistic I used to be before becoming a policeman. Having fled Afghanistan, successfully settled in Canada and accomplished so many things as a family were all because of our positive outlook on life. We saw what was possible and were able to dream about our future. Some of these characteristics are slowly ripped away from police officers as the years mount, mostly because of all the dark and disturbing things we see on the job.

Months later, I was called to the front counter of the police station where I was told that I had a visitor. As I walked out to the lobby of the police station, I see a family sitting in the waiting area and our front counter clerk pointed me toward them. As I walked toward them, I see that a woman who is having difficulty getting up is trying to stand up to come close to me. As I get closer, I realize that the lifeless body of a woman in her thirties who had laid before me a few months ago had now come to life and was trying to approach and give me a hug. She seemed to have lost a lot of weight. She spoke to me in a very soft and weak tone—even though doctors had told her to be on bed rest, she had to come into the station to thank me for saving her life. She came there with her young family and the tears in her eyes provided me with the ultimate job satisfaction. I realized that even with all the negativity that comes with police work, I needed to focus on days like this to keep me going. On this day, I also told myself that if I accomplish nothing else in this job and quit today, all the effort I put into become a cop had been worth it.

# CHAPTER 4

# Stories in understanding others

As I continued my job as a police officer, I came across many interesting and unusual situations. The unexpected surprises, the behaviour of human beings and the circumstances leading to these incidents never stopped being interesting for me. No two situations seemed the same. I learned something from almost every single one of the hundreds of police incidents I was involved in. I was left with interesting stories, memories, tears, frustration, and laughter. The ability of human beings to cause such a variety of conflicts in each other's lives made the job both challenging and interesting.

## The barking dog complaint

A barking dog complaint involved little to no effort, just talking to a dog owner about the excessive noise their four-legged friend made. The worst case was having to seize the animal if it was neglected and turn it over to animal control.

During a warm summer day, when the blue skies and the hot temperature brought everyone outside, including dogs, we received a call about a barking dog. First, I said I will just go there alone, should be no big deal. Then a fellow officer who was nearby offered to join me so we both walked up to a house in a quiet middle-class neighbourhood.

We hear the barking dog; a female answers the door and we tell her that we were called because her dog has been barking for a while and just want to make sure all is well. She invites us in and asks if we want any water, iced tea, or something cold to drink. We thank her for the offer but tell her that if there is any way she can move their dog to a different area to reduce the noise and we will be on our way out. As we are speaking with her, the husband, who appears to have been drinking, arrives and tells us to get the fuck out.

The man walked into the kitchen and grabbed a butcher knife. My colleague and I both draw our firearms out and point it at the man, ordering him to drop the knife. His wife is now yelling at us saying what the hell is wrong with us two, and to put those "damn guns" away. She runs in front of us and walks up to her husband. My partner and I look at each other in disbelief and I tell her that we had better create some distance, so we move back a bit. We call for additional help as the man runs upstairs with the butcher knife in his hand and his wife chasing him.

We freeze again—what the hell do we do now? I hear them yelling and her saying: "Give me the damn knife or they will kill you!" My partners and I can't believe that the situation has escalated from a simple check-in on a barking dog to this.

The woman somehow manages to take the knife away and throws it down the stairs as we are trying to climb them. We jump out of the way as the knife lands on the carpet. We put it away and rush up to see that the man and his wife are both okay. We put our guns away quickly and handcuff the man. When it was all over, we had no idea how or why we got to the point where our life flashed before our eyes and we were ready to shoot a man if he took a few steps in the wrong direction. These types of situations make frontline police work unpredictable and stressful. Without any information, preparation, planning, or tools, young officers are often put in these situations where their judgement—or lack thereof—has life changing consequences for them and those whom they serve.

## Interactions with the Indigenous people - why the lack of trust

It was the first time someone told me, as a police officer, to "get the fuck out of our land" and that "we don't recognize your authority." The complexities surrounding the issues between the RCMP and First Nations people go back to the formation of Canada, a sad topic for another time. As a uniformed police officer, I always felt out of place when going to a First Nations Reserve to respond to a call. Firstly, I thought the term "Reserve" was insulting. Unfortunately, life in isolated and often neglected communities where First Nations people live, raise their children, and die have only made slight improvements while the rest of the country is growing at a much quicker pace.

It was like going to another country. I only counted on my ability to relate to people and know the residents as individuals to make sure things went smoothly during my visit to a First Nations call for service. For me, driving a police car into First Nations land was much worse than walking in on foot so they could not see the car. It was a challenge to make a visit to First Nations land. The odd rock thrown at my police car, the person who would walk by and spit at the car, or those who just showed their middle finger and swore as a police car drove by always reminded me that time has not healed the wounds of the past and an RCMP car might be reminding the First Nations people of past injustices their ancestors had to endure.

Despite the hostility, I never feared going into First Nations land. As I got to know the residents as humans, I felt that they were often resentful about the lack of interest and genuine care from the police. They told me that every time they saw a police car, they were reminded of heavy-handed tactics of the past and the lack of understanding of the First Nations people by the system. They also thought that someone hiding inside their police car just driving by was cowardly. They would say to me "why don't most of your guys get out of their cars and talk to us like people? It was these types of in-person interactions that thought me valuable lessons about how to engage with the First Nations people. Interestingly, they never had the same feelings about me or some of the other officers who took the time to relate to them. I knew that their culture would never submit to this type of law and order that has kept them in a standoff with the establishment and it was unlikely to change. I understood their point of view and empathized.

After understanding how the First Nations people felt, I realized that the rock throwing, spitting, and swearing was not at me, it was at a symbol. I developed a great working relationship with the people and authorities within the First Nations; unfortunately, I was not able to do much in the way of gaining trust on behalf of the uniform I was wearing. There had been too much damage over too many years and not much to make up for it. I always wished that I had spent more time with First Nations people; however, I also knew that spending time with them as a police officer representing an institution they did not trust was not going to be very productive. This void stayed with me as one of the things I wish I had done more of as a police officer.

## What it felt like to be a street person

One of my interests while being a police officer was to do undercover work one day. However, I was never that passionate about it. Eventually I applied for and was given an opportunity to take part in the undercover training program. After years of doing the same type of work and training, most cops become predictable beings, from the way they talk to the way they dress and carry themselves. I am often surprised by how easy it is to identify a cop who is on surveillance or even if they are on their days off. You might ask why this is. I think it is the culture of police work where we become so used to working and socializing with each other that some of us had a tough time blending in with the rest of society. This is also why some cops have difficulty relating to criminals; because they see them as so different from themselves. Yet people who commit crimes are still people. I also related this to the experiences of immigrants who are treated differently, just like the experience I had as a street person; because they look different, they are thought of a certain way. I think that our eyes deceive us every day; we judge people and things just based on what we see and not think about all the complexities beyond what we see.

In 2012, at the age of thirty-eight and having been a policeman for eleven years, I was now a team leader at the homicide unit and was about to have yet another unique life experience. The undercover training course was the only time we had to use our imagination and fully immerse ourselves into certain roles. I found myself on the streets of Vancouver with a full beard, torn clothes, dirty fingernails and a look that allowed me to blend into Vancouver's downtown Eastside. Because of my previous work at the VPD jail, walking up and down the streets and alleyways surrounding the corner of Main and Hastings was familiar to me. I knew the sounds, sights, smells, and, most importantly, the people. By the way, nothing I am about to discuss here is a big secret, most members of the public, the courts, and even those involved in a criminal lifestyle are familiar with all these stories.

One of my first practical assignments was to dress the part of a functioning cocaine user and find drugs on the streets. So, I hit the streets of downtown Eastside on a mission to purchase cocaine. My job was to not be detected as a cop, safely buy the drugs and follow the rules of undercover work. My first attempt to purchase cocaine took about three minutes. I walked up to a drug runner. He looked at me and nodded his head. I used the hand signal for cocaine, which was to point my thumb up. "Up" was the street name for cocaine. He used his head to direct me to a doorway where another man was standing in the shadows. This guy was the dealer. I paid him fifteen dollars and he gave me a tiny shrink-wrapped ball of white substance. I took the drug, put it in my pocket, then walked away. This was how easy buying drugs was.

My next drug purchasing mission was like the first one, except that, this time, I had to buy heroin. I followed pretty much the same routine as the first one, except this time, I had to act like a heroin addict. I was acting drowsy and walked with limp muscles and my head down. I found a drug runner and a dealer on another street corner.

I moved my thumb in a downward motion, down being the street name for heroin. The drug runner pulled my arm and said: "Come here". When I looked at him, I realized that I had arrested him many years earlier. Like a bad actor, I was about to jump out of character because I thought this guy will for sure remember me as a cop, and if this happens, what the hell am I supposed to do? Fortunately, he is so focused on selling me drugs that he does not look at me for long and takes me to a female dealer. Next came the part that made me nervous.

The dealer has a needle in her hand. The runner tells the dealer that I wanted some down. The dealer starts to prepare a needle full of liquid heroin and asks me to give her my arm. I refuse and tell her that I want it for later. I am now worried about being stabbed with a needle filled with heroin. I then start to walk away, and the runner walks behind me, trying to intimidate me into going back. I am worried about two things. He might attempt to beat me up because I pissed them off by walking away from a deal. I also wonder if he recognizes me as a cop. I have no idea which one might be worse, but I don't know what else to do but keep saying sorry with my head down and walking away from them.

I hear the runner say: "She got the fucking rig ready for you and now you walk away, you fucking guy. Don't show your face again here, you hear me? You need a kick in the head." Now, I truly felt the pain of the drug addicted street people being assaulted. What would a person do if they were assaulted or stabbed with the needle? Can they run to the cops? The cops do not live on the streets with them every minute of every day. I realized that addicts must obey the rules of the streets or they would get hurt.

Despite my best efforts to stay low key and not attract any attention, a police officer who was doing a wonderful job of walking the beat on the Downtown Eastside noticed my behaviour as a likely drug purchaser and stopped me. All he said was: "Can we have a chat?" This officer was one of those foot beat cops who seemed to know the streets of the Downtown Eastside well, to the point where he knew who was new to the streets. He told me that he had never seen me on the streets and could tell that I was new, he wanted to know why I was walking up and down the street looking for drugs. He skillfully told me that life on the street can be very difficult and becoming immersed in the life of drug use will make life even more difficult. In a subtle way, he told me that I should probably try and get back on my feet and not come back to the Downtown Eastside no matter what was happening in my life. He explained that using drugs to cope with my troubles in life was a sure way for things to end bad. This officer was respectful, caring, kind, and seemed to truly care about the people on the streets. He and many other VPD officers exemplify this type of dedication and caring shift after shift at all hours of day and night for many years. I already had an immense amount of respect for the VPD officers who worked on the Downtown Eastside, and on this day, my level of respect for them solidified even more. This encounter also reinforced my belief that a cop who came across as a human was likely to be more effective on the job than one who looked and carried himself like a robot.

The lens through which I saw drug addicts and those who lived on the streets changed my beliefs. Up to this point, I had the misconception, just like most police officers and members of society, that if the drug addicts really tried, they had a way to get out. Well, it's not that easy. I also learned that the revolving door of arresting them, putting them in jail, and having them face the already overburdened legal system was not the answer either.

As I walked away from this drug purchase, I realized that the streets of Vancouver were as unkind and unforgiving to the addicts now as they were ten years prior. The high rises in downtown Vancouver, the billions of dollars in development, and the expansion of the city had changed the face of the Lower Mainland, but nothing seemed different for the people of Downtown Eastside. The same demographic, especially the over-representation of

Indigenous people, were facing the same struggles as they have been for decades, the same cycle playing out on the streets. I also thought about how the police and the justice system were ineffective in this case. I thought money was being wasted on the enforcement of the drug laws and charging people of Downtown Eastside with crimes. This was a public health issue wrapped in a lack of social support and little has been done to fix it.

As I went through the remainder of the undercover training course, I realized the stark differences between how I was treated as a human being depending on the circumstances I found myself in. In my duties as a homicide team leader, I was often dressed in a suit and walked the same streets to attend court, have meetings, and investigate murders. My appearance alone got a lot of smiles and courtesy from people, because they thought I must be somebody important because of the suit. As a smelly homeless person who hadn't shaved for a few months and wearing torn and dirty clothes, people were doing everything they could to avoid standing beside me, or even coming face to face with me because I was looked at as less than human. This is the heartbreak people on the streets face every day. My experience on the streets of Vancouver was an example of what plays out on the streets of many other major cities in Canada and the US. This also reminded me about the day my Dad and I were at the old Mandawi market in Kabul over thirty years ago, the images of the man who, based on his status, was abusing the older man seemed the same as the way street people were treated in Canada. I realized that human compassion is often the missing ingredient when it comes to the poor treatment of others.

## The even darker side of police work

In June 2006, I was sought out by the Lower Mainland's homicide team. I accepted their offer and changed jobs, and went from being a local cop to working in a much bigger area, as my new job took me to just about every town between Pemberton and Boston Bar, a vast area with a population of over a million people. This was the beginning of almost a decade during which I became immersed in the world of death. Being part of over 100 homicide cases, I investigated murders, suspicious deaths, child deaths, and police shootings. I saw victims at all stages of trauma, dealt with many families of murdered victims, interrogated murder suspects, completed crime scene examinations, and followed many lifeless bodies from the crime scene to the autopsy table.

I spent pretty much all my thirties living amongst the dead. Their faces, stories, and the mysteries surrounding their last moments in this world were full of challenges for me. The challenges of investigating murders were the mechanical part of the job which I became very good at after so many years. The bigger challenge, which later affected my life, was the mental and emotional impact this type of work can have on a person as a human being.

With every year that I spent at the homicide unit, the number of dead, the lives they led, and how they ended up losing their lives cluttered my mind with more stories of human tragedy. There were times where I would ask myself what the hell is the matter with me? Growing up in a war-torn country, escaping death, and finally making it into a safe country should have led me to pick a line of work that was a little more positive. Coping with some of the cases and circumstances surrounding the murders was very difficult. This was especially true in cases where human brutality was obvious in the way some victims were killed.

There are certain things that a human being witnesses in her or his life that will likely stay with them forever. The notion that police officers and others who are in the business of dealing with human tragedy on a regular basis can better cope with such tragedies is a myth. They may have a better ability to mask their emotions, put others before themselves, and focus on the job for the moment. But the emotions they feel are just as powerful, if not more so, than for any other member of society.

The distinct smells of burnt, decomposed, drowned, or buried human bodies are some of the things that will likely never leave a person's subconscious. Many homicide investigators who have spent a long time in this line of work can be easily triggered by certain smells. I believe that we carry this baggage with us for the rest of our lives despite the fact that we chose to do this type of work in the spirit of serving the public and bringing closure to the families of those who were murdered.

Fortunately, most people, including police officers, will not be able to tell you what a human corpse smells like or how it feels to be looking inside a human being on an autopsy table. This is because a very small number of people in society are exposed to murders and all the bad stuff that comes with it. I see this as a good thing. To me, the work was important and someone had to do it, and doing this job was a selfless thing for me. I did this job as a service to the public but just like most young dedicated cops, I had no idea how much it would take out of me.

As much as cops criticize American television shows about their unrealistic portrayal of how a police investigation unfolds, I found that some of the things that took place in the early hours of a murder investigation were not that different from a TV show. The chaos surrounding a murder scene, including police cars rushing to block off the area, covering the victim's body, putting up police tape to keep people away, news cameras racing to the area to get the footage of the crime scene, and detectives showing up to take over the scene—all play out just like a TV show.

Every time I started work on a murder case, the interest from the media combined with public's fascination with murders made me feel like I was on some type of TV show. The serious, fast paced, and often fascinating nature of such cases was the exciting part of the job for me, I guess these must be the same reasons murders pique everyone else's attention in society. However, what the public often does not see, once things calm down, the initial excitement is gone, and the next big story on the news consumes the public's interest, are the cops who are left with the heavy burden of carrying such cases. The long hours of work by homicide investigators and the tedious work which at times lasts years is nothing like any TV show. The passion to solve a murder case and having the patience and commitment to bring closure to the victims' families are the main reasons that kept many of us going for years as we continued to collect evidence to resolve a case.

## Murder stories

In the following stories, the facts and specific information about each case has been altered. I have done this because the purpose of these stories is not to give out a bunch of facts about specific murder cases. I am telling these stories from my perspective as a human who went through the emotions, experienced the sounds, the smells and the mental stress of what it feels like to be a human being—not just a cop.

The importance of these stories is their relationship to bigger societal and systematic issues which often cause the tragedies I am about to describe and the emotional impact on the cops. So as far as case facts are concerned, one would be able to learn much more about a murder while sitting inside a courtroom where all the facts surrounding a case play out for months. The details of the crimes are not my focus here.

Instead, I hope to highlight the human element of the heavy side of police work and the lives it touches. The legal system is overly fact driven and there is virtually no focus on the human element. I understand the reasons for this in a legal setting. Unfortunately, there is no venue for the human element to play out. Also, the societal factors almost never form part of these cases. Yet I feel that they were often some of the most important contributing factors to the actions of those committing murders. Family struggles, troubled childhoods, drug and alcohol addiction, mental health issues, and greed were often the main reasons for a person deciding that killing someone was the answer to a situation they faced. Unfortunately, our reactive and punitive society is willing to spend billions of tax dollars each year in policing costs, yet the areas which need the most money, such as mental health, drug and alcohol addition, and other societal ills, are barely funded. I feel a responsibility to tell my story as a former homicide cop to highlight what I thought were the gaps in our reactive system which focuses so much on the mechanics of crimes yet neglects the more important aspect of troubled lives, which is prevention and the human side of things.

## The case of digging up a body

It was during my first year as a homicide investigator that I was assigned the role of crime scene manager for a murder case. A man had gone missing for months and it was believed that he may have been murdered. After months of investigation, our team finally managed to catch a break and found a possible location where the victim may have been buried. Narrowing down the specific area where we could locate a human body within a large and isolated area was no easy task. Nevertheless, we found the location.

It was a sunny day in early September. As we set up our equipment along a remote coastal town in preparation to dig up the body of a person, I looked around at the scenery. I saw what looked like a great area for someone to come and spend a quiet day by the water and take in the peaceful and beautiful views. They could have a picnic on the beach, maybe start a fire by the water and become one with the calm of the vast Pacific Ocean as the tide came in at the end of the day, and maybe listen to the gentle sound of the tide getting even closer to shore as the night fell. This was a perfect place to pitch a tent and wake up to the gentle sound of the Pacific Ocean and hear sound of the birds nearby in the forest behind.

As I was staring at this beautiful area, a seasoned forensic identification officer tapped me on the shoulder and said: "I hate to disturb your daydreaming, but we gotta start digging if we are going to find that body and get the remains out of here during daylight." I was the only guy standing there appreciating the view while the rest of the team was already in their bunny suits, with masks and blue latex gloves on, ready to get to work.

The tap on my shoulder and the reminder from the forensic identification officer truly woke me up from daydreaming; this was a defining moment for me in my job as a homicide investigator. I learned that wherever this job takes me, I am there to look at the place as crime scene. I found this disturbing because I was afraid that all the places I might see in this line of work would leave me with a dark memory of whose body we recovered there and that soon, there might be too many areas that are tainted for me. I quickly snapped out of it and put my faith in the outfit I was working for and said to myself: Well, I guess if I go through tough times on the job, there has got to be people there to help, and those who have been at this for so long and those in senior police leadership positions would look after us. I decided not to worry about my feelings, I had a job to do and was not there to enjoy the view, so I got to work. I quickly geared up and was ready for the dig.

I had seen dead people before and was exposed to other types of trauma during my first few years on the job, but this was my first time digging up a human corpse. This is not the type of thing a person can prepare for. The emotions that comes with experiencing such events vary from person to person. We all have our coping mechanism, and this dictates our physical and mental reactions when it comes to dealing with the dead.

As we carefully start to examine the area surrounding the dig site, I found that my daydreaming was not exactly a fantasy. I find articles that are evidence of people picnicking, having campfires by the water, making sandcastles, and even some children's toys that were left behind. I realize that all summer long, families and children have been playing and enjoying this beautiful isolated beach without ever realizing that a human body was buried beneath them.

As we start our dig to unearth the body of the victim, we took care not to damage the remains— slowly removing the sand by hand, in small amounts, because we could not disturb the position of the body, our hands starting to cramp. We had to take small breaks just to stand up and walk around for a minute to bring the circulation back to our legs as we had to kneel to dig. The annoyance of having to go to the bathroom, fight hunger and thirst were also part of that long day. As we neared uncovering the body, almost ten hours had gone by. It was during these days that I would normally send a quick message to my wife in an attempt to say that I still remembered having a family and a home, but that I wouldn't be home anytime soon. The smell of a human being who has been buried in sand for about six months was so strong that I had to walk away several times and bury my face into the ocean water just to feel and smell something to take away the strong odour of a decomposed human body. Once we had completely cleaned all the sand from around the victim's body, I saw the trauma inflected upon him. Unfortunately for people who examine such crime scenes, looking away or just taking a quick look is not an option. No matter how much the trauma bothered me, I had to sit there and carefully examine and document the extent of injuries and the state of the victim. This is a necessary part of the job which later helped us in finding answers and recovering more evidence related to the victim's demise.

As we stretched our arms and legs from having to crouch inside a grave to uncover the victim's body, we took a short dinner break. Protein bars and water was something we always carried in the trunks of our cars for days like this. No one was in the mood to go for a drive and get food, so protein bars and water it was. I looked around and saw that most of the team members involved in this recovery were either sitting on the ground, a rock, or a knocked down tree. No one said much. I felt that we were all in deep thought while eating our protein bars and looking at the beautiful surroundings. I thought about asking everyone how they felt about this situation? What was going through their minds? Were they okay? Did any of this bother them? Although I was doing everything to buy into the way things were done, I found myself at odds with the culture of policing in Canada. Coming from a collectivist culture, I realized that these were lost opportunities which could have helped everyone there to heal from what we had just seen. Instead, the wounds scabbed over, and no one talked about how they felt and moved along to the next task, like a robot. Despite being an advanced country where human rights and stability are a given, I felt that there was so much pressure on the individual to cope with tragedies alone. This is something I felt worked to the detriment of a person's psychological well-being and eventually, the society itself would pay a heavy price for these wounded souls. I knew that the young Afghan kid wanted to talk about all that I experienced with friends, family, and colleagues because I grew up with the mentality of sharing our joy and sadness so no one was ever left alone to suffer in silence. I wish I could have been able to bring this aspect of my culture to Canadian society. It didn't happen during my career as a policeman, but it was something I did not give up on.

Unfortunately, in police culture, no one wanted to start a discussion by asking questions such as the ones above. Being one of the newest guys at this crime scene, I decided not to say anything. But I knew that this was not a healthy thing to do. How can men and women who do this type of work be expected to just keep going? I know that unless people are psychopaths, human emotions are experienced by everyone. Shouldn't we have talked about how this and many other cases affected us as humans at some point during these investigations? As the years went by, I realized that many such moments went by without any discussion. Eventually, because of the nature of this work and the police culture, I started to adapt and became numb to many of these feelings, too.

We continued to work just before the sun was about to set and moved the victim's body into the transport van. I seized the evidence related to the crime and completed my documentation. The team used the ocean water to wash up and we all packed up and left the area. The smell of a human corpse buried in the sand for over six months is unique and difficult to describe. After spending long hours in the company of a human corpse that emanated such a powerful odour, the smell got into my clothes and skin. I realized that it would take a while, but I would eventually get the smell of this crime scene out of my body. I wasn't sure if the same would be true about what had stayed in my mind from this experience.

Many more steps follow the examination of a crime scene, such as the one above. Processing the physical evidence, attending the autopsy, and completing forensic laboratory requests for the scientific examination of the physical material are some of the many steps involved in the post recovery of a victim's body.

## The case of children killing children

The ills of substance abuse, anger, and other mental conditions in murders where adults were killing each other were some of the reasons which explained many murders. However, it was rare that the victim and suspects in a brutal murder case were all so young that I thought of them as children. I don't mean children in the legal sense of anyone under the age of twelve. I refer to them as children because they were not that much older than twelve.

As I kept dealing with dozens of cases in which children's behaviour at an early age started to escalate to a level where police became involved in their lives, I realized that many other things failed before I showed up to investigate a crime committed by a young person. This was especially true in cases where a young person was accused of a serious crime. I believe that the underdeveloped brain of a child needs constant guidance and influence to help shape their patterns of thought and consequent actions, and any negative influences in their lives must be reversed by somebody to prevent them from falling victim to a life of crime.

I found out that if children are neglected on several fronts, they can commit some of the most horrific acts which would be shocking even to seasoned cops. Even some criminals whom I have spoken to about the violent crimes committed by young people have told me that what they heard about certain crimes was messed up. I never thought I would come across a case where a group of children who had been introduced to drugs and alcohol at an early age and were living desperate lives would come together in a way that they could brutally murder another young person for no reason. I thought that many things had to fail for this to happen. Parents had to neglect these children, schools would be helpless in trying to guide them, they will become alcohol and drug users, accept violence as a way of life and finally come together as a group to commit a terrible act.

Just as I had answered hundreds of calls at all hours of the day and night, I received a call just after midnight during a warm summer night. This was always the worst time to get a call from work. I would normally try to have a sense of normalcy in my personal life by winding down the nights at about 11 p.m. then trying to get to bed shortly after, so receiving a call to restart a new day with less than one hour of sleep was the worst. Eventually I got used to this sort of thing, which happened regularly for almost ten years while working as a homicide cop. Now that I think back, I don't know how I could function for twenty hours after only having one or two hours of sleep. I remember there were times where a case would become so active that I would sleep no more than four hours a night for several weeks just to keep up with work.

Just like a robot, every time I answered the call for a new homicide, I would jump out of bed to reach for my Blackberry and answer it as quickly as I could, so that I wouldn't wake anyone else up at home. I would then rush to take a five-minute shower, run to the ground floor where I had my suit ready for the next day and get dressed in under ten minutes, then walk out the door and into my police car. I had set a standard that after receiving the call, I had about twenty minutes to wake up, shower, get changed, and be in my car on the way to work. Depending on where the murder had occurred, it would take me anywhere from ten minutes to two hours to get to the jurisdiction where the murder had taken place. Regardless, I was always in a rush to get to the case because I knew how important it was to get to work as quickly as possible to give each case my best effort.

On this night, as soon as I got the call about the murder and was told that the victim was a young kid in her early teens, I realized that this would be a difficult case. The more tragic each case was, the more difficult it was for me to depersonalize circumstances, the people involved, and, most importantly, the face of the victim. This is something that often causes many front-line responders to suffer emotional damage later in their lives as such stories keep adding in their minds. This was especially true in this case.

One of the first things homicide cops usually do in the early hours of an investigation—as they set up their briefing room and prepare to work long hours—was to find a photograph of the murdered victim and post it on the board. The boardrooms we used in various police departments normally had whiteboards all around the room covering the walls. As members of the investigative team arrived to work on the case, they would look at the board to see the basic facts of the case. I entered the room where all the investigators had come together to discuss the case before getting to work. Because most seasoned homicide cops deal with many murders, they do not often show much of their emotions about each case. However, there are some cases where just walking in the room gives you the sense that no matter how seasoned the cops are, the case is really bothering them. This was one of those cases. I could see the look of sadness on everyone's faces.

In this case, I never saw the victim or even spoke with a single witness. My job was to be the affiant. The affiant is normally a police officer who can write well and is responsible for preparing affidavits for legal purposes. These affidavits are lengthy documents, usually several hundred pages. They are sworn before a supreme court justice requesting certain legal authorizations. These authorizations are necessary to allow police to do things which they need a court's permission, otherwise their actions would be illegal. As an affiant, explaining every single relevant detail surrounding the murder of this young person was my job.

Up to this point, I always thought that seeing dead bodies, attending autopsies, and speaking with the victim's family, with witnesses, and with others who were directly affected by a murder was likely the most difficult part of murder investigations. As I kept writing the story of this young person's murder, I felt like I was writing a very sad story that seemed almost fictional. I thought that most people in society would likely never believe that this kind of murder happened. It showed nothing but the struggle of young people in society and ended terribly.

I found that describing the gruesome details of how a group of young people killed the victim, the sad life which the victim had lived up to this point, and the dismal future for the suspects was a complete mess. Just by reading documents and looking at crime scene photographs, I realized that the human mind can experience situations very close to reality and can feel similar feelings if a crime is explained in detail. For me, I realized that this was like the way we constantly traumatize ourselves and our children by fixating on news headlines that tells us all the terrible things that happen everyday. Also, popular television shows obsessed with stories of crime, murder, and mayhem, video games that are essentially teaching children how to kill, and the easy availability of gruesome images on the internet are creating an awful reality for our children from a very young age. I think this reality promotes the notion that humans killing other humans is a normal thing.

In a country such as Canada, where there is no war and plenty of opportunities for lives to flourish and thrive, I never accepted the reality of children becoming victim of violence. For someone who did not see much normalcy in his childhood, I always feel that the disturbing actions of young people are a result of a collective failure by mainstream society, which exposes young people to things that take away their innocence and create cases such as the murder of this young person. So, in a great country such as Canada, I think we have much more work to do by taking care of young people from an early age, so that misguided and angry personalities do not develop, resulting in young people potentially killing each other.

## The case of murder in the family

In the summer, I often go to Vancouver's English Bay area and jog along the Stanley Park seawall. Every time I go there, I feel lucky to be living in such a beautiful city. As a homicide investigator, my phone was with me 24 hours a day. No matter what I was doing or where I was, answering the call of duty became a way of life for me. I guess I also took my responsibility of investigating murders seriously and did not want to miss a beat. After a while, working or having a day off sometimes became a blur because there were times when I got more calls on a day off than I did while I was at the office. I accepted it all as part of the job.

I had developed a set of skills that allowed me to effectively interview and interrogate those who were suspected of committing crimes. As a homicide investigator, I found this skill was valuable. However, getting murder confessions was much harder than confessions to smaller crimes. Because the stakes were so high, interviewing murder suspects required additional effort and skill. For me, the most valuable skill any police officer could have was the same they needed any time they dealt with people: they had to be able to relate to people and try to understand them as a human being first.

I was given a summary of the circumstances surrounding a murder that had just occurred earlier on this warm summer day and asked to interview the suspected killer. As I listened to the facts of the case, I realized that I had learned many techniques to conduct successful interviews when a stranger had killed another. These techniques usually involved understanding a person's psyche and trying to find a common ground which allows the interviewer to relate to them and empathize with them to get a conversation going. As an interviewer, it was also easier to build a rapport with a suspect if I could try and understand their hate for the victim, which ultimately resulted in their actions. This was solely to develop a rapport with them and get the suspect to talk about the crime and eventually admit to the facts.

In this case, I found it difficult to use any of techniques to build a rapport with the suspect because he had killed his mother. I found it extremely difficult to try and relate to someone who was accused of such a terrible crime. This is not to say that some murders were not terrible; they were all difficult cases. But in this case, I struggled much more. I grew up thinking that motherhood was one of those sacred, untouchable things. There is an old saying which I have heard many times in the Persian culture, it goes something like this: paradise is under the feet of mothers. I always accepted this because of how much a mother goes through for the sake of their children. In a short moment, the sacrifices this mother must have made during pregnancy, birth, sleepless nights, and years of taking care of a child until they were capable of looking after themselves flashed before my eyes. How could a child forget all this? How could they not know? Then I had to compose myself and get to the task on hand. So, I relied on my gut instincts and tried to put my judgement aside while trying to understand this young man as a person. I was pessimistic in this case.

I started the interview with this suspect by following the usual steps of explaining his legal rights, learning as much as I could about him, and attempting to keep him talking and interested in spending time with me. I found that the actions of this person were mostly driven by anger, so I had to find the source of that anger. He had some substance use issues, some type of a mental condition, and was living a life that he hated. I found that the combination of life circumstances left this young man hating himself, and he had never found a way to channel his anger.

The only person whom he could find to place blame on was his mother. Unfortunately, the displaced anger against his mother was entirely unjustified. Those he should have been angry at were the people who introduced him to drugs and alcohol, forced him into living a lifestyle where he felt used and worthless, and the lack of resources in dealing with his mental health. His mother could not have helped him in any of these areas, especially after he became an adult. I found that he felt powerless against those who were truly responsible for negatively affecting his life and making him feel like a worthless human being. I felt that the evildoers in this young man's life had the power to cause all the damage yet were not affected by his violent actions at all. His kind and caring mother was the unfortunate soul who fell victim to his rage because she just happened to be there.

This was one of the many cases where I found that so many things in this young man's life and around him failed for many years. The substance use and abuse had taken part of his control and affected his judgement, the culture of young people being exploited by the criminal element to profit from their vulnerability had driven him to a demeaning life style, and the lack of mental health resources had worsened his state of mind. These had collectively produced a young man who was looking at himself as worthless and who was volatile.

As I spoke with this young man and learned more about his life, I realized that if he wanted drugs, there were many people who could easily sell him drugs. I know that because if I could buy drugs in three minutes at the corner of Main and Hastings, then so could he. If he wanted to drown himself in alcohol, he could find a liquor store on almost every street corner of the city. However, if he wanted to find a place to seek help for his mental health, where would that be? Did he live in a society which made it so easy for him to destroy himself and very difficult to put his life back together? I think so. It was these types of cases which made me feel that there is a huge gap in addressing the root caused of why people become criminals. Mental health professionals, addiction specialists, and counsellors are constantly begging for funds while crime fighting and any other fear-driven professions get all the funds they want. I feel that other cultures have much more to offer Canadian society in this aspect. If a person is addicted to drugs or becomes desperate in life, what can help them is having a family and a community who rally around them and support them both mentally and financially in an attempt to take care of them. I feel that these days, it has become too easy for people to write off their family members and quickly walk away from them because they may be troubled. I feel that this does not reflect a healthy society where individuals are left to struggle on their own during some of their darkest moments in life.

I realized that after a few hours of talking to this young man, my cloud of judgement began to lift. I did not forget that he was suspected of killing his mother and that my job was to get him to talk about the murder and collect the facts. However, I could easily see that even a terrible crime like the one he was suspected of committing has its complexities and reasons. In the end, the young man did admit to me that he killed his mother and the details of the brutal crime. However, just like all the other confessions, this only answered the question of why this happened and not what can be done to prevent it from happening again.

I often walked away from these interviews with mixed feelings. On the one hand, I felt that I had accomplished my job as an interviewer, but on the other hand, I was, as always, stuck on the human element of the case. This was the most difficult part of all the interviews I conducted with murder suspects, because I almost always managed to connect to the human being. This left me with a sense of sadness as to why this person had been failed. In this case and many other cases, the suspects were failed by external factors, so they lashed out in a horrible way, destroying another life and that of their own.

## Murder in the concrete jungle

Part of my job as a homicide cop was also to investigate institutional murders. Every time I heard someone suggest the use of prisons as a tool to control crime, I knew that they had no idea about what life inside a prison was like. For many years, I had visited various federal and provincial prisons in Canada. Mostly I was there to speak with one of the inmates and within hours I would be out of there. It wasn't until I spend a few days inside a prison that I appreciated the true nature of life in jail.

It was during a warm summer afternoon that a group of inmates at one of the institutions decided to kill one of their own. Prisoners had used sharp objects, referred to as shanks, made from anything the prisoners can find, to stab the victim and then beat him to death. During the investigation, I learned the inner workings of prisons and how difficult it was to spend time in such a place. Murder scenes were almost always gruesome, and a murder inside a prison, where the victim was beaten and stabbed to death by a group of inmates, was extra gruesome. The excessive blood on the walls, doors, and the marks showing that the bloodied victim was dragged so that he could be beaten further showed me that there was an added brutality about murders inside a prison.

Bad behaviour by a group of inmates often results in the lockdown of the entire institution. Prison staff explained to me that when things become tense for any reason, the safest thing to do was to lock everyone in. However, they did their best not to impose this because of the hardship it caused the inmates. Because of this incident, the entire institution had gone into lockdown mode, and no one had been able to leave their cells for several days. As we combed the entire prison for evidence and interviewed dozens of inmates, I found myself feeling at odds with the notion of incarceration. From years of investigating serious criminal offences, I knew that the justice system had no choice but to incarcerate most of the inmates because of the crimes they have committed, yet I could not help myself but feeling sad about looking into the eyes of those who were peering through their little cell windows with bars just to see if they could find out what we were doing. Most of them were trying to strike a conversation with us by asking how much longer they would be stuck in their cells especially because most had nothing to do with the murder.

What struck me most was not that a group of inmates had brutally beaten one of their own to death over a minor dispute, but how the human condition and the environment can truly bring the worse in some of us if we are put in a place like a prison, where a person's daily survival becomes a struggle. As I met many of the inmates while interviewing them, I realized that those who had spent ten, twenty, or more years in prison could no longer relate to people in the outside world. It was a strange experience, like meeting people from a different era who were still living in the past. By talking to them, I got the sense that time stood still for them and they experienced little to no change inside the institution. The routine of having their meals, getting some fresh air, and the few things they did inside the prison to keep them engaged was all they had, and this repeated itself day after day for years or, in some cases, for decades.

Comparing prison life to the outside world, where an overwhelming number of things happen daily, especially in today's fast-paced world, makes is almost impossible to think that a prisoner who has been locked up for so many years can ever function in the outside world. I saw how prisons are the worst place for humans; they destroy the human spirit and produce more harm to society than good.

For many years, I believed that prisons could serve as a place where inmates can be rehabilitated. Unfortunately, my opinion of prisons, after spending only a few days inside and speaking with a handful of prisoners, left me with a dismal view of rehabilitation. I felt that a human being's capacity for understanding, for compassion, to bring positive contributions to society, and all that is good slowly disappears inside a prison. It was these prison visits which made me change my mind about why it was so important to make sure that prisons should be a place of last resort, especially for those who have not committed crimes against a person.

Despite our best efforts to gather evidence to solve this prison murder, no one wanted to cooperate and tell the cops anything. They all gave me very good reasons. They said, Why should we tell the cops anything? Will the cops be there when we get cornered inside the prison and called a rat by other inmates? Will the cops stop the other inmates from beating us or stabbing us while we try to make it though each day inside this concrete jungle? And my answer to all of them was no. As I learned about the rules of prison, it became evident that the smallest things seemed to be a big deal to those who lived inside this concrete box. Inmates would fight over food, television programs, toilet paper, and just about everything. Most of us on the outside world have no concept of what goes on inside a prison.

An inmate told me that once, a young man who had just gotten into prison was whistling and he was warned by others that if they heard him do this again, he would be in for a beating. I was puzzled by this, but the inmate told me that prisoners think that only birds are free to whistle and in jail, no one if free, so you don't whistle. This and many other small things about life in prison stayed with me forever. Society's interest in the business of law and order, courtroom dramas, cop shows, and prisons has produced many television shows and movies that depict these things well. However, I feel that no one really has a true understanding of how things are unless they spend some time up close and see the sights, hear the sounds, and smell the odours to appreciate how life is for some humans who find themselves in prison.

Protecting society from harm by incarcerating human beings who can harm others makes sense. However, after seeing how these humans live and treat each other inside a prison, I felt at odds with the purpose and existence of prisons. Could there be a better way? I know that in places like northern Europe and countries such as Holland, prisons are struggling to stay in business because they have decided that jailing people is not the way to keep society safe. The scary but opposite is true in North America, where the prison industry has been a booming business.

I certainly do not have all the answers, but I know that in a country like Canada, we can do much better than to follow the ineffective model of imprisonment used in the US. I know that our limits as human beings are tested every day and that if we could control our thoughts, words, and actions towards each other, then as people we can find a better way to resolve our differences. Resorting to crime and victimizing each other to the point where we accept prisons as a necessary part of our society cannot be the only way in a civil society.

# CHAPTER 5

# The meaning of being a cop

## The things they don't train cops for

One of the assumptions made by most young and naïve cops, or even by seasoned cops who just don't get it, is the notion that just because they are a police officer, everyone must respect them. Those who understand people realize very quickly that this is not the case. Some of the best cops I ever worked with were those who could talk to people comfortably using everyday language and put their cop hat aside. Yes, they had to be professional and follow the rules; however, there was a lot more to be gained by being a genuine person with those whom we interacted with than to just spit out dialog like a pre-programmed robot.

Some of the bonds I formed with people who were part of my professional life were with those who were convicted of serious criminal offences, such as multiple murders. I felt that there was a certain degree of humanity and compassion which I displayed towards those who I felt were dealt a very bad hand in life. I still thought that they had to be held accountable; however, I also felt that some of these people were just not the winners of life's lottery.

As I met these people during interrogations or jail visits, I realized that some of them had too many negative things stacked up against them from a very early age. Life just did not give them a chance to recover from one struggle before they found themselves in the middle of another. They went from one bad situation to another and crime became a part of their life because following rules and living a legitimate life almost became impossible for them. And so, they became immersed in the criminal subculture. It is hard for most people to understand that once someone's life becomes like this, it is all they know. Getting a job, quitting drugs, leaving all your friends and associates, and even moving to a different part of the country are often difficult things to do for those who have never done anything in their life which fits the norms of society. So, being able to relate to those whose lives are anything but ordinary and normal was both a challenge and a reward for me.

At times, it was hard to shake hands with someone who had killed a human being with their hands either by stabbing, strangling, or shooting. Yet I found a way to see past this as a professional and try to make sense of why humans are pushed to these extents. I always felt that a human being who had done terrible things should be judged and held accountable, but not by me. I looked at it this way: How are they interacting with me? Now that the person is in trouble, what is my job? I never took pleasure in punishing anyone. Despite my belief that everyone should always be held accountable for their actions, I always felt a sense of sadness about anyone going to jail who genuinely showed remorse for their crimes. I felt that jails were built for those who had no heart and showed no remorse for hurting others, a place to go when there was no hope left.

As I met more and more people who were stuck in the criminal sub-culture, I developed the professional relationship that I was warned about many years ago. Someone once told me, Don't ever become someone's personal cop, because they will become a pain in the ass and call you with every stupid little problem they have and think that you are their cop friend. Just do your job and walk away. Fortunately, I never took this advice. I encouraged people to call me and I would be there to help them when I was on duty. If I was not working, I would make sure that someone else helped them.

For me, being a cop was not just about dealing with people as objects. At times, I became people's personal cop because they trusted me, and surprisingly, no one ever wasted my time. Those involved in the criminal sub-culture contacted me many times because they needed help or guidance. I took that as a compliment because they remembered me as a caring cop, someone they could call to seek help from if they needed to. Unfortunately, the lack of trust in the police is one of the worst things about a society or a system. The police officers who gained the public's trust were those who held the integrity of this job intact.

## Not keeping up with the times

Because of the reactive nature of police work, we were always behind in training, technology, and, most importantly, understanding our ever-changing demographics and societal issues, such as the way each generation lives and thinks about what is important to them. For this I don't blame the cops who, for the most part, must follow policies and established rules, so there is not space for their creativity. I think it is the vision of some police organizations that makes it hard for police officers to relate to the people they serve.

After spending many years in the RCMP, I acknowledge that their image is an important part of Canada's history and a recognizable symbol. Canada Day parades, musical ride displays, bringing the Stanley Cup out to the ice are all nice displays and symbolic roles of this organization. However, when it comes to practical and operational needs of communities in today's Canadian society, these symbols don't do anything. This bothered me because I felt that Canada, the country that welcomed me and so many others, the country with such amazing values, deserves to be represented by the RCMP in a better way.

Many communities across the country have been frustrated for decades about the Ottawa-led organization the heavy bureaucracy of which prevents timely actions to address community issues at a local level. I kept hearing from many outside agencies we worked with that once the big red machine gets involved, everything will be slowed down because things can only be done the RCMP way. And they were right about this. This also added to the inability of those who tried leading the new generation because the organization was moving so slow in a time where almost everything happens instantly. In my view, the RCMP has a lot to learn from other police agencies and the private sector across Canada and they need to do this urgently because they are way behind. Having to obtain multiple levels of approval which causes lengthy delays by the time things go from the province to Ottawa and then back, waiting months or sometimes years to make changes to forms, business rules, technology needs, and other things which need to change urgently are some of the many setbacks people face working under such a system.

## Challenges of being an effective leader

As I progressed in my career, I was promoted several times, first to supervisor, then team leader and, later, to team commander. At each level, I had to accept that I had to overcome the constant conflict I had with the organization. The organization was mostly focused on protecting their image and I was more concerned with treating people well, then worrying about the organization. I realized that relating to people and understanding them as humans was key to developing a strong team and leading people. This was at times contrary to the teachings of an organization that puts loyalty to the company first and keeps the employees in line to ensure that, above all, the organization's interests are protected. The challenges surrounding working in an environment such as this are many. As a leader, I found it difficult to navigate my way through these issues. I always went with my instincts of supporting the humans first.

To me, leadership was an innate ability and, from my perspective, there was a mixture of both good and bad leaders in the RCMP. I always felt that, as an organization spending billions of dollars in public funds, they could not afford to have bad leaders, and they could have done a much better job in developing good leaders and remove those who have no business being leaders.

Unfortunately, the RCMP's philosophy was that everyone could be a good leader if they were taught how to lead. This is something that added to my frustration year after year as I saw ineffective leadership development programs unfold and was disappointed by the lack of value they placed on education and incorporating knowledge from outside organizations who operated much better than they did. I was also disappointed to see that very few leaders had the courage to do the right thing even if it meant that they would be criticized and not supported by the organization. This was especially true as it related to identifying and addressing human resource issues and dealing with those who were problem employees. Other than being afraid of lawsuits, resistant to change, hard-headed, and stuck in the past, I did not know how else to take the attitude of this organization.

The years that I spent in leadership positions were made possible because I had the support of some good senior leaders. I know that from time to time, they were criticized by the organization for the way they operated, but I knew that change in the RCMP was slow and someone had to keep challenging them to effect meaningful change.

To be fair, I must divide RCMP management in two categories. Those who had strong operational backgrounds, knew the human side of things, had a high level of emotional intelligence, and operated based on a strong set of solid principles were among the good leaders. The others were what I call the paper cops, the ones who barely contributed to public service, always took the easy way out, and their most noticeable skill was to talk about themselves. Their decisions often reflected a lack of emotional intelligence, and, in my view, this was damaging to the RCMP and a disservice to the public.

## My contribution to my country as a Canadian

As I neared almost two decades of being a cop, I realized that it was time for me to contribute to public service in another capacity. I wanted a new challenge and became frustrated with the RCMP which was going in the wrong direction and would eventually fall apart. I had to keep reminding myself that police work was bigger than the organization I worked for. I also could not lose sight of the support I had from those who were good leaders and recognized my efforts. I received over a dozen certificates and commendations for outstanding service and the medal of meritorious service. I no longer display these awards in my office as I once did, I only keep them in a folder as a reminder that these were gestures of appreciation by the good leaders on behalf of the public whom I served.

I had to look at the number of people I met and the lives I touched just because I found myself interacting with Canadians during some of the most difficult moments of their lives. This gave me the sense of purpose, and I think the same is true for most cops.

My unconventional ways of working, and especially my way of interacting with others, including those caught up in a criminal lifestyle, raised many eyebrows in a culture where uniformity and conformity is expected from everyone. I knew that at times, I was looked at as a rebel. My convictions about doing the right thing for the right reason stood above all.

On a positive note, I experienced camaraderie, taking risks together to protect the public and being part of something bigger than myself with those who were genuinely good cops. I think being a cop was a great chapter in my life because I got to serve my country and meet so many great people whom I can share interesting stories with for the rest of my life. I also feel that my life was enriched because of everything that I experienced on this job. The bad stuff will be hard to forget, and this is the price I paid for being a cop. However, I try to make the best of it by thinking that even the bad stuff gives me a unique window into people's lives. This is something that most members of our society will never see.

# CHAPTER 6

# Life after being a cop

After spending such a long time in police work, I knew that I had to strive for a more balanced life. I knew that it would take some time to transition back to normal life. It was during this time that I thought a lot about all my cop friends, their families, and the difficulties they endured because of this job. I did not think it was my place to convince others to leave the job sooner than the normal twenty-five, thirty, or, for some, even thirty-five years of police work, but I knew that for me, it was the right thing to do.

I asked myself the questions, When will they leave? How much more negativity will they experience? What price would their families pay? And, lastly, how healthy will they be once they retire after spending a life time doing police work? I had no answers and I also knew that I could not go to them all immediately and convince them to do what I had done. By this time, I kept hearing about those who retired from police work and, within months or a few years, either suffered a stroke, a mental breakdown, or, in a few cases, had killed themselves. How can their lives end like this? Something was wrong with this picture.

It became one of my missions that, after stepping away from police work, I would be an advocate for uncovering the truth and ensuring that not just cops but all those who give so much to public service are not eventually discarded and forgotten. I also knew that it was important for cops to know that the other side of life exists, the side that some of them had forgotten about because the job was all consuming for them.

Despite leaving a public service job, I knew that I still had a lot to contribute to society. I decided that no matter what I chose to do, I would not stop working in an area where I help people. After being through all the ups and downs of police work, I knew that I had to find a way to continue to help others, but I did not want it all to be full of negativity and judgement.

I knew that my life struggles and circumstances had taught me many valuable lessons, yet I needed further spiritual and personal development and growth to move on to the next phase of life. At this stage, I began to ask myself questions about the constant lack of harmony in the world and I no longer wanted to believe the good versus bad and heroes versus villains notion of life.

I knew that, from this point on, I must devote my professional life in an area where a compassionate understanding of the world in a global sense, which forms the core of my belief system, was complemented by working in a field where I could help heal people from mental and physical ailments. My decision to move away from police culture was highly beneficial; it allowed me to begin clearing my head from the negativity of the world I had been part of for a long time and see the world through a different lens, a lens where I could help people live better lives.

I learned that, after each significant juncture of my life, there were important lessons and things that I took away which served me well and helped me understand life and the world a little better. For many years, I categorized my experiences and life events as both good or bad ones. However, as I became more mature and tried to understand life at a deeper level, I realized that our life events cannot always be looked at as good or bad, they are just life events and each one teaches us a lesson. It is the meaning that we decide to attach to these events which make them good or bad in our own consciousness. This was an important realization for me at a time where I had to accept the reality of losing those whom I loved dearly as part of life's events.

## Family and the meaning of life

Despite all the challenges that we endure in life and the tragedies we see unfolding all over the world, I always believed that having a family and children is an important part of life. Yes, it would be hard work to raise a family and worry about their present and future needs, but I always thought about my parents. Somehow, Mom and Dad raised four children under challenging circumstances, so what was my excuse for not having a family?

In 2003, I met someone whose life story was not that different than mine. Her family had come to Canada from Iran around the same time as we had come from Afghanistan, and we grew up more or less the same. I realized how much we had in common. We were born in two neighbouring countries, speak the same language, and have many of the same customs and traditions, as both our home countries were once part of the Persian Empire. Both our families were forced to flee our homeland due to war. Yet, decades later, we met in Canada, a country thousands of miles away, while speaking English to each other. For some reason, the minute I started to speak with her, I felt at ease, and in my heart, I knew that this was going to be a lasting relationship.

Two years later, we got married and since then, we had a great deal of experiences which enriched my life in many ways. I fell in love with her even more as the years went by and I realized how positive, genuine, caring, honest, and loving she was. This hasn't changed until this day. During our travels to various places in Canada and the US, and overseas to Mexico, Cuba, France, and Italy, we realized how similar we were in wanting to understand and appreciate other cultures as much as we wanted them to do the same for ours. We connected with people as humans despite being able to only speak a few words of the language in the country we were visiting at the time. Our values were further cemented to such an extent that, no matter where we land in this world, we can be at peace with others and put them at ease with who we are if we genuinely tried to connect with them. There were always places where we felt uncomfortable and met people who were prejudiced, but they were few and we tried to see the world from their limited perspective. This helped us stay positive and not amplify the few unpleasant experiences we had.

The part of my personality which had become rigid because of my job as a cop was not an easy thing to live with. My wife made many sacrifices because of what I was doing to make a living, yet she stood by me despite all the challenges. Her non-judgemental and accepting nature as a person who always sees the good in others taught me a lot about tapping into my inner self. I found that I valued and wanted the same personality traits to come to the surface for me. One of the biggest reasons that I was able to walk away so easily from being a cop was my wife's support.

Over the decade and half of being married at the time of writing, we had three wonderful children. The luxuries and privileges of life afforded to our Canadian born and raised kids often reminded me of children in other parts of the world. I often struggled with trying not to compare life in Canada versus those in other parts of the world who were lacking the bare necessities. With the help of my wife, we tried our best to raise well-adjusted children and use kindness and compassion in understanding the world from their perspective. After all, just like any other Canadian kid, they didn't know anything about what takes place in other parts of the world and the hardships other children endure. This was a difficult topic to deal with. On the one hand, we did not want to raise spoiled kids, and on the other, we had to understand their reality and not make them feel bad about having a better life. My wife and I decided that we would inform and educate our children about what happens in the world yet not overwhelm them with this topic at a young age. So daily gratitude and appreciation for the small things in life became part of our life.

As our children played and took interest in various toys, movies, popular shows, etc., they often asked me what were my favourite toys or shows when I was a child. I had to find ways to explain to them that children who grew up in war don't often have too many memories about play or toys. Because peace and security were missing, the primary concern for most kids growing up in a war-torn country is having a peaceful country. I had to find creative ways to communicate with my children about how I grew up. As I was about to witness the process of these new lives flourishing in Canada, my father was getting older and nearing the end of his journey in life.

# The impermanence of life

By the age of eighty, my father was living a quiet and peaceful existence. I think he lived in a meditative state for many years towards the end of his life. Dad had become quieter than usual, especially after he visited Afghanistan in the mid-2000s and saw the city of Kabul reduced to rubble and the significant deterioration in the living conditions of our fellow Afghans. Dad described the state of the country as being much worse than it had been during the war with the Soviets. I knew that, upon his return to Canada, Dad often thought about those whom we had left behind yet he knew that there was not much we could do to change their lives.

Dad had become even more grateful about our life in Canada and seemed at peace with almost everything around him. He continued to remind us about the importance of family and peace. From time to time, he reminded us about our struggles as a family and everything that we had lived through to make sure that we did not lose perspective, especially if he ever saw us worked up about trivial things that bothered us in our lives as Canadians.

After living a long life full of challenging circumstances, Dad no longer complained about anything. When he suffered heart failure at the age of eighty-two, he told my mother that he had some chest pains in the middle of the night, but that he did not think it was a good idea to call an ambulance because they were busy with more important things and maybe he could just wait to see if the pain just went away. Mom called the ambulance anyway and saved his life.

While Dad was mostly quiet in the final years of his life, he was still a tower of strength for us. His presence alone added to the richness of our lives as our family grew and Dad met six of his grandchildren. On the day Dad was taken to the hospital for the last time, I could see the look on my mother's face. She knew that this time, he may not come back home. Mom was a strong woman; I never saw her break down and she always remained composed to ensure that we were not worried. But this time, I knew that she was really upset.

As I started hospital visits with my Dad, my four-year-old son insisted that he wanted to go to the hospital and cheer up his "baba kalon" which means grandfather in Farsi. I took my son to Dad's bedside and despite Dad lying in a hospital bed and not feeling so well, he sat up as soon as he saw his grandson. Dad created room for my son who asked him if he could jump up and down on the cool bed for a minute. Then he made Dad smile by saying "Baba kalon, I have some jokes for you." We spend about fifteen minutes with Dad on that day and my son asked him if he could come back and see Dad again. Dad said: "It may not be a good idea for you to come to the hospital anymore, I don't want you to get sick."

In less than ten days, Dad stopped talking, eating food, or drinking water and his body started to shut down. As we gathered around Dad's hospital bed during his final days, he had a constant smile on his face. The doctors and nurses would come in to ask him how he was, and his answer was always the same: "I'm ok." Just two days before he died, one of the attending physicians spoke with me and said: "I know your Dad keeps saying that he is ok, but just to let you know he will likely be gone within the next two days." I told the physician that I knew Dad was nearing the end of his life, but the reason he keeps saying that he is ok and has a smile on his face is because he has lived an incredible life and is at peace with leaving this world. Dad had always told us that life was just a transit stop in a bigger journey and as such, we should always be ready to leave. He taught us the most important lesson as a family: to never get attached to worldly things, because they are just things. When it is time to leave the world, the things stay behind.

As I looked at Dad in his final days, my belief in being a good person and living a simple and honest life became clearer to me than ever before. I thought about how humans come to this world making so much noise, and how some continue to make noise their whole life and even cause others to suffer, yet when we leave the world, we leave so quietly and without any of the material things or accomplishments we have accumulated. I feel blessed for having a father who was so at peace with leaving the world. He had lived a simple life and never became attached to material things or accomplishments. For me, the final lesson from my father's life was that in the end, we have to say a final goodbye to what we hold as the dearest part of this life, our family. With this mindset, it was very easy for me to become the type of person who can let go of things.

I knew that my father was the type of person who made the best of every situation and he was no different in his final days. I knew Dad's taste in music, so during our hospital visits, I would play calm Afghani music and American music from the 50s and 60s. Until he stopped talking completely, he would still make the odd comment about how I understood good music, and I would tell him that it was thanks to him and our culture, and how grateful I was to maintain this as part of my life. Then, just to test his memory, he would name the artist and names of the songs. I was amazed at his sharp memory at this late age and the state he was in. It was during these moments that I appreciated the gift of meaningful lyrics and music even more. The service that artists provide to humanity with their music was priceless.

We stayed with Dad around the clock for the last ten days of his life. We saw him go through each phase of letting go of life. My sister, who is a year younger than me and lives in the US, had flown to Vancouver to see Dad, and never left the hospital. She told me that she felt a sense of relief in Dad's face as he saw her and kissed her head and smiled at her, as if he was waiting for her to show up in his final days to say goodbye. My younger sister also told me that she witnessed Dad holding my mother's hand and smiling at her, then telling her that he hoped she forgives him for anything which he had said or done during their life together which may have been hurtful. Mom responded by saying, I always have. My mother and father had always told us that no matter what your religious beliefs are, one thing which is important to remember is that in life, we will likely do or say things that could hurt others, and that it is ok to make these errors as we are humans. The important thing is that you should always ask for forgiveness from the person and not God. This is something that God will not do. Being married for forty-three years to my mother, they had the normal arguments, but they always worked it out. So, I felt that Dad wanted to make sure that even in his final days, him and mom were ok. This is an example I hope to follow in my life.

Dad first stopped eating because he knew that his body could simply not process food anymore; two days later, he stopped drinking water because he did not want to use the bed pan. The next day, he closed his eyes and was just breathing. On the last day, my mother and sister had spent all night at the hospital and the rest of us had just arrived at the break of dawn. As soon as we parked our car at the parking lot of Royal Columbian Hospital, I got a message from my sister who said that Dad was just about to take his last few breaths. We gathered beside his bed, and Dad took his last shallow breaths, then there was silence.

Our hearts felt heavy, yet for some reason, all of us were at peace. I was raised in a Muslim country and our family believed in spirituality. I don't ever remember associating religion to anything extreme or fanatic in our home. To us, being part of any faith or spiritual belief simply explained that there was a higher power than us. I never liked getting into debates about belief systems because I know that there are over seven billion people in this world and no one has all the answers. If there was such a thing, then everyone would believe in one thing. I relied on our faith as something which reminded me of three principles, which were repeatedly spoken to me by my father: live a simple life, be grateful for all that you have, and don't forget that we are all destined to depart from this world. The verses of the Quran from Surah Yasin were playing on one of our phones placed near Dad. The last verse of the Surah Yasin was most fitting as we listened to it being recited in Arabic: "So exalted is he whose hand is the realm of all things, and to him you will be returned" (approximate translation). I believe that our Dad went towards his next journey, I have never been able to fully understand what that journey may be, but I guess this is the best part. I'll find out once the time comes. At that moment, I thought that when the day comes, I hope to die this way, too.

We buried Dad according to Islamic tradition. Prior to the burial my younger brother and I took part in the preparation of my Dad's body. In our tradition, family members of the same gender who are able and willing often assist the professionals at the Mosque with preparing the departed person's body for burial. A final bath, application of pleasant scents and wrapping the departed in a sheet of cotton and saying a prayer are the main steps to this process. I found that this process helped my brother and I learn one more lesson as men about the circle of life. We found it therapeutic and it was an important step for us toward accepting death as part of life.

After the Jenaza (a final prayer at the Mosque) where the congregation who were present for the Friday prayer stood behind Dad's casket and the Imam performed the service, we followed Dad's body to the cemetery. As I looked around the green and quiet cemetery, I saw all the faces surrounding us. Young and old, men and women from our Afghani community whom we had known for decades. Many of them shared the same story as our family, escaping a war-torn country to come to Canada and live a more peaceful life. In addition, those who had become part of our family in Canada from other backgrounds, faiths and cultures were also present.

I saw that our almost thirty years of living in Canada had blessed us with being surrounded by a rich mix of people from all corners of the world who had come to pay their respects. Dad's funeral was blissful. There was nothing extravagant about it, a sense of calm and the clean spring air surrounded us as we were about to lay him to rest.

The quiet reflections of everyone standing still and the recitation of the Holy Quran from one of our community elders gave me and our family a sense of peace and closure. We were able to let go of Dad easily knowing that we were returning his body to the creator and his spirit had moved on to experience things that are beyond this world.

The day my brother and I laid our father's body, wrapped in a single sheet of cotton as per our religious beliefs, in the ground, the impermanence of life became a reality. Dad's words to us echoed louder than ever as he laid there silently: Do good while you are still alive and let go of worldly attachments, because life will go by very fast and there is nothing worse than regretting things you could have or should have done that you can no longer do.

After going through the passing and burial of my father, I think I reconnected to my roots a bit more. I realized that despite being a Canadian and living life here, I must cherish my upbringing, culture, and spiritual beliefs. I realized that I drew most of my strength from the values I was taught during my formative years and this was what helped me stand on solid ground during difficult times like this. It was during this time that I also reflected that our family had been away from Afghanistan for a long time, and this time and distance meant that we would not likely be there to console each other when a loved one passed or to celebrate the birth of new lives. Every few years, we heard about a relative passing away or a cousin having a new baby. During our first decade of living in Canada, the situation in Afghanistan was terrible and we could barely communicate with anyone. With the improvement in technology, we were able to contact family members a little more frequently than we had been able to for years. Despite this, our family accepted the reality that our life was now in Canada and we would only be hearing from a far distance about the births and deaths in our family whom we left behind three decades ago.

For many months after my Dad's passing, I often thought about the past and our journey as an immigrant family. I thought about how different each person's life can be depending on which part of the world they were born in and what life had planned for them. The lack of our control over what might happen in the future and accepting the past as part of history and letting it go became evident to me. I could see that the life I lived was very different than the lives our children will live because of their environment.

I count myself lucky to have lived a life where I was able to witness the birth of my children. Laying my father's body in the ground was an experience that made me appreciate life even more. I think these types of experiences help us maintain perspective on life. By seeing the birth of my own children and laying my father to rest, I believe that I was able to witness the complete circle of life in the purest way.

Bari Emam

## Canada's compassion - a sense of pride

Almost thirty years after our family left a war-torn Afghanistan, I think that we settled into a life in Canada where I never wanted to see helpless people from another country go through the same despair the Afghans went through.

In 2015, the refugee crisis created by the war in Syria brought me back to the days where our family was living in uncertainty and seeking safety because of war. I closely followed the news about the world's reaction to this crisis. As this story was unfolding, I saw a disparity between the countries all around the world and could not help but judge their reactions. I was proud to be a Canadian and encouraged by the response from countries such as Canada and Germany, amongst others, who agreed to accept large numbers of refugees to respond to this humanitarian crisis.

I remembered that thirty to forty years ago, the US called Muslims who fought the Soviets in Afghanistan freedom fighters and rebels, praised them for their bravery, and welcomed them in large numbers to their country. However, in 2016, islamophobia and the ignorant attitudes towards Muslim people was abundantly clear in the US and some other parts of the world who were too scared of Muslims. It seemed like the politics of fear had blinded many people in some countries who turned their back on the Syrian refugee crisis. They focused more on ensuring that their people lived in fear than to help those caught in a humanitarian crisis. Lifting the dark cloud of judgement seemed unrealistic at this time, as many Syrian refugees were not allowed to enter some countries.

As human lives were being lost in Syria, I could also see the efforts of Canadians. Despite some groups who were trying to play the politics of fear, the true spirit of Canadians came out and crushed this unnecessary fear. Again, I was proud to be Canadian and could see that my country did its part in helping the Syrian refugees. Accepting tens of thousands of refugees into Canada and helping them settle into our country affirmed my belief that I truly live in a compassionate country and among humans who are kind to each other and to those around the world.

The few acts of hate towards the Syrian refugees by ignorant and racist individuals in several Canadian cities were disheartening. However, the amount of support, compassion, and effort to make the Syrian refugees feel welcomed to Canada was truly amazing. I kept hearing that government agencies were overwhelmed by the offer of support from Canadians who were willing to assist refugees. The spirit of volunteerism among Canadians and their ability to see past the ignorant and fear-based attitudes of a few reaffirmed my belief that our country is going in the right direction.

As I came across some of the Syrian refugee families who were settling in the Greater Vancouver area, I could see the similarities between their adjustment and struggles to fit into their new homeland and that of our family three decades ago. I was encouraged to see that, by far, most Canadians were helpful and welcoming towards these new members of our society. As I came across these families and saw their children enjoy a peaceful life, it reminded me how quickly humans can adjust to the conditions presented to them. Just like us, these young children lived in a state of unrest and under constant threat of violence just a few months before and now peace and prosperity has opened the door for a better future.

# CONCLUSION

As an immigrant from Afghanistan who did not speak more than a few words of English when our family landed in Toronto on a cold and crisp day thirty years ago, I feel that Canada is where I belong. Our struggles as an immigrant family made me into a survivor and Canada gave me the opportunity to explore my potential. I am proud of the work I did as a police officer and the opportunity I had to come face to face with Canadians in some of the most challenging moments of their lives.

Although I now feel that I am a Canadian first, I will never forget where I came from. I say this because despite three decades of being away from Kabul, I am still connected to those we left behind. I take joy in their happiness and become sad when they are struck by tragedy. At the time of writing, a suicide bomb claimed the life of one of my second cousins who lived in Kabul. He was in his 30s. Stories like these are part of everyday life for immigrants who have fled war-torn regions of the world.

I ask every immigrant to use the diversity of their life experience and culture as a source of strength and to make their mark in a positive way by becoming a part of the fabric of Canadian society or any other country they now call home. And I ask every Canadian to recognize the strength and richness of those who have come to Canada from all corners of the world to contribute. Canada is a wonderfully unique country because of its rich diversity. In most major Canadian cities, we can see all the different shades of humanity and, for the most part, we all live together in harmony. This is only possible because of the effort every Canadian makes to live in a peaceful society.

We need to see the contributions immigrants make and recognize their passion and effort in making our country better. The challenges of multiculturalism are many; however, the ethnic backgrounds we came from, how we got here, the lives we lead, and our differences should never stand in the way or divide us. If you look at every human, in the end, we are all the same. We come to the world the same way, live our lives in a variety of ways and then we go back the same way. Reminding ourselves about this part of humanity is important so we don't lose perspective and the purpose of this life.

I walked away from the cop world sooner than I had originally planned because it was an important step to ensure that the job did not define who I was. This is a phenomenon among those who spend several decades of their lives in a line of work which is all consuming. Police work is one of those lines of works where just because we chose to do this job, we had to accept so many restrictions on our daily life for the sake of being a cop. Despite all this, we still need police officers, and someone must do the job. I just hope that by telling my story, I have raised awareness about how cops look at the world, and not let the job dictate how they can live their lives. They need to take this responsibility in their own hands and keep a positive world view, while remembering that their job is important, however, it is not their life and they are just playing a role for the time that they are a cop, it should not define who they are as a human being.

Society's expectations from cops by looking at them as those who would act and live as exceptional human beings is also part of the change needed to make lives easier for the cops. The public will only have a realistic understanding of their police officers if they are informed about how cops are hired, trained, treated daily by their organizations, and the situations they encounter on the job. After all, billons of dollars of taxpayer funds are dedicated to policing, so it is only fair that the public knows the truth. I hope that in this book, I have provided an understanding about some of the things cops go through on the job and how it affects their lives and that of their families. I also hope that as someone who is different than most Canadian cops, I was able provided a different perspective.

Now that I am a parent of three and as I reflect on my life's experiences, I am beginning to live life over again through the eyes of my children. I see purity, simplicity, compassion, forgiveness, and unconditional love from these little persons. Their perspective is much better than mine; despite my optimistic view of life, I still think that I have been looking at life with a polluted mind. All the good and the bad experiences in life shape our thoughts about the world. I feel that these thoughts add to the baggage we carry during our lifetime and that the load gets heavier as we move on through life unless we become aware. Most of us have been paying a heavy price for getting caught up in the world of accomplishments, judging others, and forgetting the basics. I feel that children at a young age are free from this burden. I am now learning some of the best lessons about life from my children and I find this to be an incredible experience. I have never been more aware of the simplest things in life which I now consider are the most meaningful and important ones to cherish.

I want Canadians to know that despite the hardships many immigrants have endured in their homeland, they come to Canada and contribute in significant ways and go above and beyond. Think of it this way; immigrants are not here to vacation, most of us have come here to do our best and be the best at whatever we do even if it causes us further hardship. Please value immigrants as humans, respect their culture and the values they add to this country. So before judging others who have come to this country from all corners of the world and may seem or act different than the norm, please ask yourself the following questions: Do we truly know them? And do we appreciate what they have been through? These are simple yet meaningful questions we must all ask ourselves as it will shape the future of our country and the direction we are going as a nation.

I can say for certain that the awful memories and life experiences of many immigrants has shaped who they are, but do not define them. Let us see immigrants in the context of here and now. Most of them want to leave all the negativity behind and appreciate the opportunity for a second chance in life. It is unlikely that the discussion surrounding immigration and how the world responds to it will ever go away.

I am hopeful that the spirit of human compassion and positivity will become a central theme of how the world will respond to the ongoing refugee and immigration crisis. It is this spirit that can give rise to celebrating diversity, embracing other humans at their time of need, and allowing them to grow and contribute in a positive way. I know this is possible because we were able to successfully integrate into Canadian society and I remain hopeful that this will be the case for most. The alternative is the divisive politics designed to inflict fear into people's thoughts. This fear-based view of immigrants will only drive those who are displaced from their homelands to take the destructive paths of division and hatred which will given them a dismal view of their new homeland. If this happens, then how can they trust anyone in their new homeland? This cycle can repeat itself for many generations to come, causing countries to remain divided.

My life experience as a child who grew up in a war-torn country, lived as a refugee in a foreign land, witnessed the despair of people in Vancouver's Downtown Eastside, and was a distant observer to the Syrian refugee crisis in recent years has led me to conclude that human struggle will likely remain part of life. However, I do not accept that we can stand by and watch our fellow humans suffer while we do nothing. Pretending that none of these struggles are part of our life creates the illusion that we live in a bubble. I believe that the struggles of others are also a part of our lives. By extending compassion and understanding, we have a chance to respond to others in need in a better way. This is what makes us human.

My passion to contribute to the greater good led me to seek a second career that still involves helping others, yet this time I chose to enter a field that focuses more on helping people heal from their wounds and not focusing so much on blaming. After spending almost two decades of reacting to incidents, I realized that the focus on prevention and self care was one of the biggest things missing in the lives of most people who found themselves in desperate places. I'll put it this way: it is better to stop someone at the edge of a cliff and hold their hand to show them the way back to life than to suggest that you will be there to catch them at the bottom if they decide to jump.

I learned both from personal experience and by observing others that we have the ability to create our own present and future experiences. I chose to take on further graduate level training in psychology. I always knew that our minds have an incredible ability. We can heal from past wounds by letting go of the things that no longer serve us and work towards creating a hopeful future. This can only be accomplished if we know how to use the power of our minds. I began this new journey to further educate myself and have the necessary knowledge to help others live a positive and optimistic life. Most importantly, I set out to show people that life is full of hope and if we can train ourselves to see life in this way, then the rest will come easy. The dream I once had to become a psychologist is now within my sights. Because I have the support of a loving family and call Canada home, I feel privileged to pursue my next calling in life. As the Buddah said, there are only two mistakes one can make along the road to truth; not starting and not going all the way. So, I started this next journey and am committed to going all the way with it. My goal for the future is to help reduce human suffering.

Canada is stronger when we come together and connect with each other at a human level. Our differences may be many, but the most important thing we share with each other is that we are all humans. So, let's show this in the way we live amongst each other, how we treat each other, and teaching the next generation everything we can about unity and oneness.

I will end this book with a verse of a poem written by the late Taranasaz (an amazing Afghan poet and song writer) and performed by the legendary Afghani artist Haider Salim, who has dedicated most of his life to producing meaningful songs. The poem is in Farsi and is about zindagi (life): "Na zindagi o na een ab o dana memanad, fakad ze nek o bade ma neshana memanad". It can be translated as: "Not this life, nor the water and seeds of it will last. The only imprint we leave behind is our good and bad [actions]". These days I often find myself listening to such songs, as I have chosen to keep life simple and accept it as a short phase of our overall journey as living beings.

# AUTHOR BIOGRAPHY

Bari Emam was born in Kabul, Afghanistan. He was fifteen years old when his family escaped the war-torn country in the late 1980s. Arriving in Canada in 1990, Bari only spoke a few words of English. About ten years later, after completing high school and several years of post secondary education, Bari's passion to help others led him to become a police officer.

Bari believes in working hard and never giving up. He made the most out of every opportunity as a Canadian. In the first fifteen years of his career as a police officer, he was the recipient of ten different awards, including for Outstanding Service, Lifesaving, and a Medal of Meritorious Service from the Lieutenant Governor of British Columbia.

Bari also completed a Bachelor of General Studies and a Master of Arts in Criminal Justice at the University of the Fraser Valley. He continues to have a passion for learning and helping others and is nearing the completion of further graduate studies in pursuit of a second master's degree in psychology. He strives to increase understanding between Canadians and those who are new to Canada, helping them see that they are not all that different from each other. Bari believes that we are all connected as humans and as such, are all part of this country's fabric. Bari believes that unless we continue to advocate for a fair treatment of all people and create a just society, our future will be in grave danger. Bari refuses to believe that the innate goodness of humans can ever be defeated by the destructive forces of hatred and fear. For the next chapter of his professional career, Bari's goal is to contribute to social justice and stand against all forms of oppression and discrimination. He will be an advocate for diversity and fairness. Such issues required an ongoing conversation informed by our intellect and influenced by our hearts where compassion and the spirit of human connection is at the center.

Bari, his wife, and their three children live in the Lower Mainland of BC.

# BACK COVER DESCRIPTION

*If you knew where I come from and what I have been through,
you will understand who I am.*

If we focus on the human connection, our lives will be enriched. If we understand the struggles of others, it might humble us and give us a different perspective. Unless we hear someone else's story, how can we ever get a different perspective? It is through these stories that we gain a sense of appreciation about what type of people we share the world with.

From growing up in a war zone to almost spending two decades of my life as a police officer in Canada, I have a unique and extraordinary view into human lives. Differences between people in various parts of the world are often highlighted. Yet, I believe that despite all the perceived differences it is our commonality that is the key to understanding each other. No matter what part of the world we call home, human struggle is part of life everywhere. Despite the struggles in our lives, it is our attitudes which determine our destiny.

Rare acts of violence around the world create fear and promote the illusion that our way of life is constantly under threat. Amplifying and embracing the core values of humanity such as compassion, kindness, understanding, and self-responsibility will paint a more complete picture of what is happening in our world.

As a child, I witnessed the destruction of my birthplace. Over thirty years have gone by and Afghanistan is still not peaceful. Despite all that goes on in our minds, immigrants try to live a normal life, maintain a positive outlook, and remain hopeful that the next generations will experience less turmoil.